THE RIVER

OTHER YEARLING BOOKS BY GARY PAULSEN YOU WILL ENJOY:

THE VOYAGE OF THE *FROG*
THE WINTER ROOM
THE MONUMENT
THE COOKCAMP
THE BOY WHO OWNED THE SCHOOL
THE CULPEPPER ADVENTURES
THE CASE OF THE DIRTY BIRD
DUNC'S DOLL
CULPEPPER'S CANNON
DUNC GETS TWEAKED
DUNC'S HALLOWEEN
DUNC BREAKS THE RECORD
DUNC AND THE FLAMING GHOST
DUNC'S LAST STAND

YEARLING BOOKS/YOUNG YEARLINGS/YEARLING CLASSICS are designed especially to entertain and enlighten young people. Patricia Reilly Giff, consultant to this series, received her bachelor's degree from Marymount College and a master's degree in history from St. John's University. She holds a Professional Diploma in Reading and a Doctorate of Humane Letters from Hofstra University. She was a teacher and reading consultant for many years, and is the author of numerous books for young readers.

For a complete listing of all Yearling titles, write to
Dell Readers Service,
P.O. Box 1045,
South Holland, IL 60473.

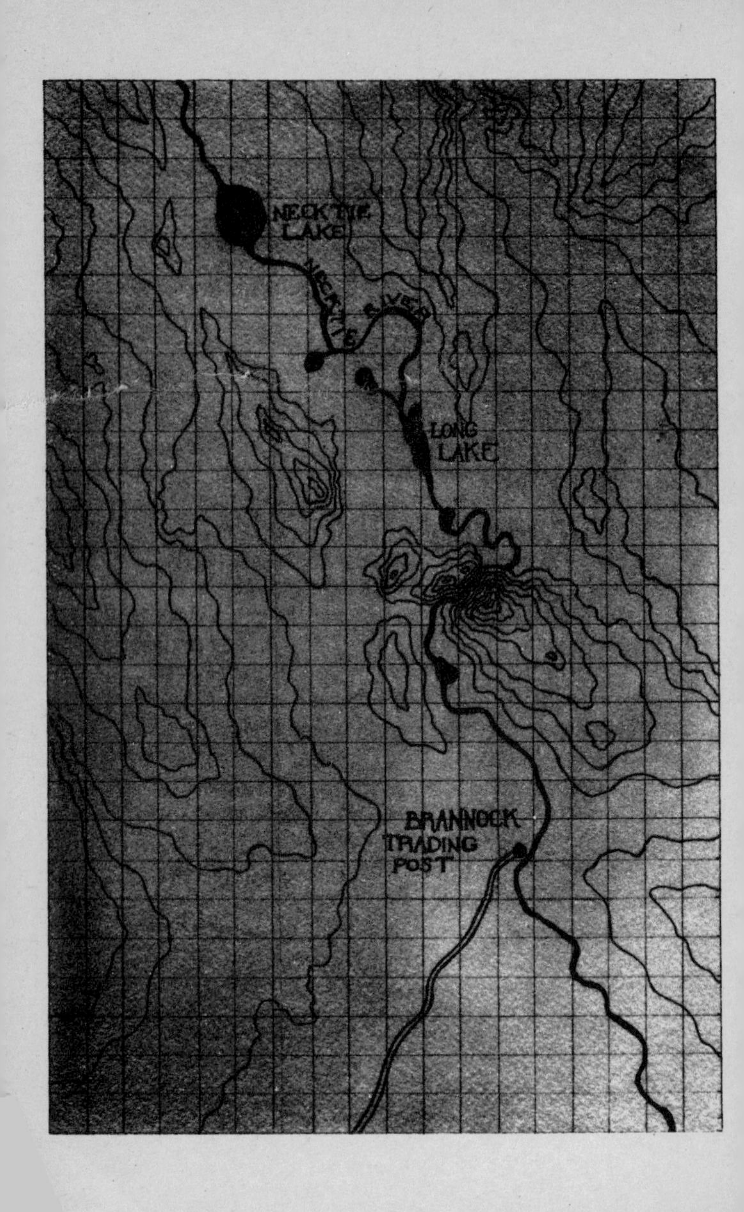
NECKTIE
LAKE
NECKTIE
RIVER
LONG
LAKE
BRANNOCK
TRADING
POST

THE RIVER

GARY PAULSEN

A Yearling Book

Published by
Dell Publishing
a division of
Bantam Doubleday Dell Publishing Group, Inc.
1540 Broadway
New York, New York 10036

Map by Neil Waldman

ISBN: 0-440-21958-2

Reprinted by arrangement with Delacorte Press

Printed in the United States of America

June 1995

10 9 8 7 6 5 4 3 2 1

To my daughter, Lynn, with love

1

Brian opened the door and stood back. There were three men, all in dark suits, standing on the front porch. They were large but not fat, well built, with bodies in decent shape. One of them was slightly thinner than the other two.

"Brian Robeson?"

Brian nodded. "Yes."

The thin man smiled and stepped forward and held out his hand. "I'm Derek Holtzer. These other two are Bill Mannerly and Erik Ballard. Can we come in?"

Brian held the door open to let them come in. "Mother isn't home right now. . . ."

"It's you we want to see." Derek stopped just in the entryway and the other two did the same. "Of course, we'll wish to speak to your mother and father as well, but we came to see you. Didn't you get a call about us?"

Brian shook his head. "I don't think so. I mean, I know I

didn't, but I don't think Mother did either. She would have said something."

"How about your father?"

"He . . . doesn't live here. My parents are divorced."

"Oh. Sorry." Derek truly looked embarrassed. "I didn't know."

"It happens." Brian shrugged, but it was still new enough, just over a year and a half, to feel painful. He mentally pushed it away and had a sudden thought of his own foolishness. Three men he did not know were in the house. They did not look threatening, but you never knew.

"What can I do for you?"

"Well, if you don't know anything about any of this, maybe we should wait for your mother to come home. We can come back."

Brian nodded. "Whatever you want . . . but you could tell me what it's about, if you wanted to."

"Maybe I'd better check on you first. Are you the Brian Robeson who survived alone in the Canadian woods for two months?"

"Fifty-four days," Brian said. "Not quite two months. Yes—that's me."

"Good."

"Are you from the press?" For months after his return home, Brian had been followed by the press. Even after the television special—a camera crew went back with him to the lake and he showed them how he'd lived—they stayed after him. Newspapers, television, book publishers—they called him at home, followed him to school. It was hard to get away from them. One man even offered him money to put his face on a T-shirt, and a jeans company wanted to come out with a line of Brian Robeson Survival Jeans.

His mother had handled them all, with the help—through the mail—of his father, and he had some money in an account for college. Actually, enough to complete college. But it had finally slowed down and he didn't miss it.

At first it had been exciting, but soon the thrill had worn off. He was famous, and that wasn't too bad, but when they started following him with cameras and wanting to make movies of him and his life it got a little crazy.

He met a girl in school, Deborah McKenzie. They hit it off and went on a few dates, and pretty soon the press was bugging *her* as well and that was too much. He started going out the back door, wearing sunglasses, meeting Deborah in out-of-the-way places, and sliding down the hallways in school. He was only too glad when people stopped noticing him.

And here they were again. "I mean, are you with television or anything?"

Derek shook his head. "Nope—not even close. We're with a government survival school."

"Instructors?"

Derek shook his head. "Not exactly. Bill and Erik are instructors, but I'm a psychologist. We work with people who may need to survive in bad situations—you know, like downed pilots, astronauts, soldiers. How to live off the land and get out safely."

"What do you want with me?"

Derek smiled. "You can probably guess. . . ."

Brian shook his head.

"Well, to make it short, we want you to do it again."

2

Brian stared at him. "It's a joke, right?"

Derek shook his head. "Not at all—but I think we should wait for your mother to come home and talk to her and your father. We'll come back later."

He turned to leave and the other two men, still silent, followed him to the door.

"Just a minute." Brian stopped them. "Maybe I didn't understand what you said—let me get it straight. You want me to go back and do it over again? Live in the woods with nothing but a hatchet?"

Derek nodded. "That's it."

"But that's crazy. It was . . . rough. I mean, I almost died and it was just luck that I made it out."

Derek shook his head. "No. Not luck. You had something more going for you besides luck."

Brian had a mental picture of the porcupine coming into

his shelter in the dark, throwing the hatchet and hitting the rock embedded in the wall and getting sparks. If the porcupine hadn't come in and he hadn't thrown the hatchet, and if the hatchet hadn't hit the rock just right, there wouldn't have been sparks and he wouldn't have had a fire and he might not be standing here talking to this man now. "Most of it was luck. . . ."

"Let me explain what I mean."

Brian waited.

"We teach what you did, or we try to. But the truth is, we have never done it and we don't know anybody who has ever done it. Not for real." He shrugged, his shoulders moving under the jacket. "Oh, we do silly little tests, you know, where we go out and pretend to survive. But nobody in our field has ever *had* to do it—where everything is on the line." He looked directly at Brian. "Like you."

The one named Bill Mannerly stepped forward. "We want you to teach us. Not from a book, not from pamphlets or training films, but really *teach* us what it's like. So we can teach others more accurately."

Brian smiled. He couldn't help it. "You mean take a class out and show them what I did?"

Derek held up his hands and shook his head. "No. Not like that. Nothing phony. We haven't worked it all out yet, but we thought one of us would go with you and stay out there with you, live the way you live, watch you—learn. *Learn.* Take notebooks and make notes, write everything down. We really want to know how you did it—all the parts of it."

Brian believed him. His voice was soft and sincere and his eyes were honest, but still Brian shook his head. "It wasn't like you think. It wasn't a camping trip. I lost weight, but more than that, I didn't come back the same." And, he thought, I'm still not the same; I'll never be the same. He could not walk through a park without watching the trees for game, could not *not* hear things. Sometimes he wanted not to see, not to hear everything around him—noise, colors, movement. But he couldn't blank them out. He saw, heard, smelled everything.

"That's what we want to know. Those things." Derek smiled. "Look, don't say no yet. Let us come back and talk to your mother, explain it all, and then you can make a decision. All right?"

Brian nodded slowly. "All right. Just to talk, right?"

"Just to talk."

The three men left, and Brian looked at the digital clock on the table in the entryway. It would be an hour before his mother got home. He had some studying to do—it was the end of May and there were finals—but he decided to cook dinner.

He loved to cook.

It was one of the things that had changed about him from the time when he was in the woods. He thought of it as the Time.

Just that. The Time. When he was speaking quietly to Deborah about it—he'd tried to tell her of it, all of it, including the moments when he tried to end himself—when he spoke to her about it, he always started it with just those words:

The Time.

A year had passed, and in the world around him not much had changed. His mother still saw the man, though not as much, and Brian thought it might be passing, what they had between them. The divorce was still final—and would probably remain so. He'd gone to visit his father after the Time and found that he'd fallen in love with another woman and was going to marry her.

Things ground on, a day at a time.

But Brian had changed, completely.

And one of the things that had happened was that now he loved to cook. There was something about the food, preparing the food, looking at the food—there was so *much* of it compared to what he'd had in the woods. He enjoyed taking the food out, working with it and cooking it and serving it and eating it. Chewing each bite, *knowing* the food, watching other people eat. Sometimes he would just sit and watch his mother eat what he had cooked, and once it bothered her so much that she looked up at him, a piece of sauteed beef on a fork halfway to her mouth.

"What is it?"

"I'm just watching you eat," he'd said to her. "It's something—eating. Just to see somebody eat. It's really something."

"Are you . . . all right?" she'd asked. Of course, he wasn't—or maybe he was and had never been all right before in his life. But he'd smiled and nodded.

"Sure, fine . . ."

But it was more that he couldn't tell her what was wrong, or even if anything was wrong—he couldn't really talk to anybody about it because nobody understood what he meant.

His father and mother had insisted that he go to a counselor when he first came back, and more to humor them than anything else he went, but it didn't help. The counselor thought he was somehow mentally injured, somehow harmed, and the truth was almost the exact opposite. He tried to tell the counselor that he was more than he had been, not less—not just older, not just fifteen when before he had been fourteen, but more. Much more. But the counselor didn't understand, couldn't understand, because he hadn't been with Brian in the woods during the time. The Time.

"I discovered fire," Brian told the counselor.

"Well, sure, but you're back now—"

Brian had stopped him. "No. You don't understand. I truly *discovered* fire—the way some man or woman did it thousands and thousands of years ago. I discovered fire where it had been hidden in the rock for all of time and it was there for me. It doesn't matter that we have matches or lighters or that fire is easy to make here in the other part of the world. I truly and honestly discovered fire. It was a great thing, a very great thing. . . ."

The counselor had sat behind his desk and smiled and nodded and tried to know what Brian was speaking about, but it wasn't there—he couldn't.

And that became the way of it for Brian. In all his dealings with the new world around him since he was reborn in the woods—as he thought of it—he had to be evasive, hold back. If he told the truth, nobody believed him; and if he was silent—which he found himself becoming more and more—they thought he was sick.

He couldn't win.

He took two pork chops out of the freezer and thawed them in the microwave. Then he found the cookbook and flipped to the page for breaded pork chops.

When he first returned home, he found himself wanting to eat a great deal. He would buy a hamburger, eat it, drink a malt, then think immediately of buying another one, but that only lasted a brief time. His stomach had shrunk and the food made him feel heavy, wrong somehow, and he'd stopped overeating.

But he still took great pleasure in food, and he now prepared the pork chops slowly, enjoying himself as he worked.

He cut the fat off them, breaded them, preheated the oven, and put them in a glass pan. While they were baking he looked at the clock again—his mother was due in less than half an hour and she was never late—and put two potatoes on a plate to bake in the microwave. He wouid start them when she came home—they baked in a few minutes—and they could eat before the men came back.

3

"It was a wonderful meal," his mother said, leaning back from the table and smiling, "as usual."

Brian nodded. "Something I whipped up."

They cleared the table. They had become strangely closer since his return. So much of the divorce, and the other man, had bothered him, but coming close to death in the woods had led him to understand some things about himself and other people. He realized that he was not always right, was, indeed, often not right, and at the same time he found that others were not always wrong.

He learned to accept things—his mother, the situation, his life, all of it—and with the acceptance, he found that he admired her.

She was trying to make a go of it alone, working in a real estate office selling lots, and it was rough.

"We have to talk," he said, putting the dishes in the dishwasher. *To have dishes, he thought, just to have dishes and pots and pans and a stove to cook the food—it still marveled him.* "Some men are coming over to talk to you."

"What men?"

He explained Derek and the other two, what they wanted.

"You mean what they *said* they wanted. They might be anybody. We should call the police."

He shrugged. "If you want. I was a little worried at first, but they didn't do anything and they seemed all right, so I told them to come back."

She thought it over and finally nodded. "Let's see if they come—we'll play it the way it looks best."

As if on cue the doorbell rang, and she went to the door with Brian following.

Derek stood alone on the front step. He backed away so they could see him well through the peephole in the door.

She opened the door.

"Hello. I'm Derek Holtzer—"

"My son told me about you. Weren't there two others?"

"We thought one man might be less pushy. They stayed in the motel."

"Please come in. We'll have some coffee."

Derek followed her in and they sat down at the dining room table and Derek explained to Brian's mother what he wanted—all that he had told Brian.

"We would control the operation closely," he said, "and take every precaution possible. Of course, we wouldn't do anything without your permission, and Brian's father's as well," Derek concluded.

His mother sipped coffee and put the cup down carefully. Her voice was even, as if talking about the weather. "I think it's insane."

Brian half agreed with her. In all the time since his return, he had had dozens of kids and not a few adults say how much they would have liked to do it—be marooned in the woods with nothing but a hatchet. But they always said it when they weren't over a block and a half from a grocery store, usually in a room with lights and cushions on a couch and running water. None of them had ever said it while they were sitting in the dark with mosquitoes plugging their nostrils or night sounds so loud around them they couldn't think.

To want to go back was insane.

And yet.

And yet . . .

Yet there was this small feeling, a tingle at the back of his neck as his hairs went up.

"I know it sounds strange, but Brian has had a unique experience," Derek said. He set his cup down carefully on the saucer. "It could save lives if he would help us."

"It's still insane." Brian's mother shook her head. "I don't think you have the slightest idea of what you're asking. You must realize that for the time Brian was gone we thought he was dead. Dead. We were told by experts that he couldn't possibly still be alive and then we got him back. Back from the dead. And now you're asking me—his mother—to send him back out there?"

Derek took a breath, held it, let it out. "Don't you see? That's exactly *why* we must do it. Because he was thought to be dead and lived, because he did something nobody else could do and if he could share that with us, show us, take us through it with him—he could save others who are in the same place. It's not just what he learned about survival—we know most of that. Or at least the survival instructors do. It's his thinking, his psychological processes, how his mind worked for him—that's what's so important."

"I have to do it." God, Brian thought—was that *my* voice?

Both of them looked at Brian. Derek in surprise, his mother with a stunned look on her face.

"What?"

Brian leaned back. "I know, Mother. But he's right. I . . . learned something there. About how to live—I mean how to *live.* And if it could help others, I have to do it."

"There is money," Derek said. "We can contract him and the government will pay well for his help."

His mother was still staring at him, but he knew, Brian knew, that she understood. There was much between them since he came back, much understanding. She treated him much more as an adult and she understood. Still, she held back, and the worry was alive in her face. "Are you sure—absolutely certain?"

Brian sighed. "I have to—if it will help others."

She nodded slowly, biting her lower lip. But she nodded. "I'll have to call his father," she said. "He may say no."

But Brian knew.

He was going.

4

It was strangely easy for him to get in the bush plane. Brian had thought at one time that he would never get in a small plane again, and when he went to visit his father after the Time it had been hard to enter the plane. But now he clambered in and took the seat in back with a relaxed attitude—it all felt the same and yet different somehow.

Derek got in the front and sat next to the pilot and turned to Brian.

"Are you uncomfortable flying?"

Brian shook his head. He looked out the window at his mother standing by the station wagon. They were at a different small airport, but it was the same station wagon with the phony brown wood sides. She waved when she saw him turn to look, and he waved and mouthed "good-bye" so she could see it.

The pilot started the engine and Brian jumped a little with the noise, but he settled back down at once.

He still could not quite believe that he was doing it, felt as if he were half in a dream. It had been two weeks since Derek first came to him, and in that time they had made detailed plans. After Brian had further convinced his mother and worked on his father over the phone, Derek had come back with maps and plans and they had included Brian's mother in the whole process.

Derek had decided he should be the one to go—even though he had little or no survival knowledge—because he was a psychologist and that was the aspect they wished to learn about.

They picked a lake in the middle of the wilderness, perhaps a hundred miles east of the lake Brian had crashed into the first time. Brian's mother thought of using the same lake, but Derek vetoed it because they wanted it all to be new to Brian. The lake was not named on the map, though it fed a river that went south and east until it disappeared off the map.

"We selected the lake carefully," Derek said, circling it with a felt-tip pen while they sat in Brian's dining room. "It has the same kind of terrain as the lake you crashed into, and roughly the same altitude and kind of forest."

"How far is it from help?" Brian's mother asked.

Derek smiled. "We'll have a radio, and if any trouble develops we can have a plane there in three or four hours. Please don't worry."

"But I do worry, that's just it."

She did worry, Brian thought, watching her as the plane taxied out to the runway. She did worry. Again he watched her get smaller and smaller and again he flinched with the noise of the engine throttling up and again he was amazed at how easily the plane slid into the air and flew.

And he was suddenly afraid.

He couldn't help it. His breath quickened and he looked up front at the pilot and thought, here it is again: one pilot and one engine and if either of them quit they were going down. If the pilot died, if he died and Derek couldn't fly, there would be nobody up front to control the plane. Brian would have to lunge over him and grab the wheel, try to get his feet to the rudder pedals. . . .

He shook his head. Easy now, easy and easy and easy. Breathe deeply, fight it. Memories of the crash came sweeping back into his mind. Mental pictures of the plane crashing down through the trees and into the water—the blue-green water, with the dead pilot next to him—suddenly filled his thoughts.

He pulled a long breath, held it, and fought the pictures away. After he'd returned home there had been dreams. Even after he had flown again, going to visit his father, there had been dreams. Not nightmares so much as reliving dreams of the crash and his time in the woods.

The Time.

But now it was different, all different. He looked at the pilot and saw that he was much younger than Jake had been —so young that he had a cassette recorder held with duct tape to the dashboard of the plane and was listening to rock music with a small set of headsets, his chin bobbing with the music. He flew loosely, slouched in the seat, his fingers lightly on the wheel, and something about him, the way he sat and moved with the music, relaxed Brian.

He eased back in the seat and looked out the window. Down and to the right he saw the amphibious float with the wheels on the side. They would land right on the lake, but the pilot could also take off from solid ground.

The floats didn't seem to slow the plane very much, as big

as they were, and they skimmed over the trees until the pilot gained enough altitude to make them seem to slow down.

Derek was silent, looking out the side window, and Brian realized it was the first time the man had been silent for as long as he'd known and been with him. He had asked endless questions of Brian.

He'd read all the stories about Brian's "adventure" (as he put it), had all the news stories on tape, and seemed to have memorized everything that happened to Brian.

"When you ate the chokecherries," he would say, "how long did it take you to get sick?"

Or, "Did you notice any changes in the way you went to the bathroom?"

"Oh, come on," Brian had said.

"No, really. All these things are important. They could save lives." And his face would get serious. "This is really, really important."

Brian realized then that Derek truly cared. Until that moment, sitting in the dining room at his house with maps all over the table—until that moment Brian wasn't sure he was still going. He had said he would, thought he would, but he wasn't totally certain until he'd looked at Derek's face and realized that Derek really wanted to help people by learning what Brian knew.

So, here he was, in a bush plane heading north. And it somehow seemed perfectly logical, perfectly all right. As if going back were the most normal thing in the world.

He looked out the window, down past the float on the right. They had been flying half an hour and they were already getting over forest. There were still some farms here and there, but less and less of them, even as he watched. When he looked ahead of the plane, through the whirling propeller, he saw the endless trees stretching away to the horizon.

With the fear gone, or controlled, something about the forest drew him; and that was a surprise as well.

His thinking had changed during the time he was at the lake. It had to, or he would have died. He had to revert, to become part of the woods, an animal. But when he came back, and had been back a time, he started to "recitify," as he thought of it. He became used to the city again. The first time he went to a mall he became ill, dizzy with all the movement and noise, and to make himself normal again he went back to the mall again and again until finally it didn't bother him.

And the woods slipped away. The dreams came less and less and he began not to think about them. He didn't forget them—he knew he would never forget them—but he didn't think about them as much; and when he did, there wasn't any fondness.

He remembered the rough parts.

The mosquitoes. Tearing at him, clouds of them, the awful, ripping, thick masses of the small monsters trying to bleed him dry.

"What was it like?" His mother had asked him one day when they were sitting in the kitchen. "What was the main problem—the worst part of it?"

And he thought at first of mosquitoes, started to tell her about them and shook his head.

"Hunger."

"Really?" She had seemed surprised. "I thought it would be the danger, or being alone, or the weather."

"I don't mean hunger like you're thinking of it," he had told her. "Not just when you miss a meal and feel like eating a little bit. Or even if you go a day without eating. I mean where you don't think you're ever going to eat again—don't know if there will ever be more food. An end to food. Where you won't eat and you won't eat and then you still won't eat and finally you *still* won't eat and even when you die and are gone, even then there won't be any food. *That* kind of hunger."

The outburst had made his mother sit back and blink, but he meant it. The hunger was the worst, worse than the mosquitoes, worse than any of it.

Hunger.

He looked out the window again. Only forest below now, forest and lakes and the plane droning. The air was rough, rougher than he remembered from before, but he didn't mind the jolting.

They had left the runway in northern New York in the early morning, but climbing had brought them into the bright sun and it warmed the inside of the plane until it was hot.

Brian was wearing a T-shirt and a baseball cap with a picture of a fish on the front. He pulled the brim down and turned away from the sun. As he turned he saw the equipment in back of the seats.

There was enough for a small army, and it bothered him and he couldn't pin it down—how or why it bothered him.

It just felt wrong.

Derek had gone over the list with his mother. Food for weeks, tent, a rubber boat, first-aid kit and mosquito repellent, fishing gear, a gun—a gun. Just what we need.

"Just for emergencies," Derek had explained. "In case we need them—we have everything we need."

And there it was, he thought. They had everything they needed and it ruined it all, made the whole trip worthless. It wouldn't be the same.

He tapped Derek on the shoulder and the big man turned in his seat.

"Too much," Brian yelled over the noise of the engine.

"What?"

"Too much stuff." Brian pointed over his shoulder at the mound of gear.

But Derek misunderstood and nodded and smiled. "Great, isn't it? We have everything but the kitchen sink."

Brian shrugged. "Yeah. Great."

But it ate at him. What they were going to do proved nothing. They were playing a game and it struck him that Derek did that—his whole life was that. He knew it was unfair to think of the man that way—he didn't, after all, know him very well. But he acted that way. Like it was all a game and Derek was approaching this whole business that way. Just a game. Football. Soccer.

If it didn't work right, they could call time out and eat a good meal and go swimming and sail off into the sunset in the rubber boat shooting things with the gun and talking to people on the radio.

Survival.

Right.

The plane seemed to hang in the sky over the woods, the trees green like a carpet out and out, and Brian sat there and watched them without seeing them and thought that it was wrong.

There was too much.

It was all wrong.

5

He slept.

He couldn't believe it, but he slept. The sound of the plane's engine and the warm sun and the sameness of the green forest all combined to hit him like a hammer, and his face went against the window and he slept.

The sound of the plane engine changing sound—decreasing in pitch—awakened him, and he was embarrassed to see that he had drooled in his sleep.

He wiped his chin.

They were going down.

Brian felt himself stiffen when the plane nosed down. He couldn't help it. But the descent was gradual and controlled and even. When they were still well above the forest, the pilot slowed the plane still further and dropped the flaps. The plane almost seemed to stop in the air, floated on down toward the lake below and to the front, and Brian remembered the last time he'd "landed" on a lake in a bush plane.

If he'd known about flaps or how to use them, he wouldn't have been going half the speed when he hit the water. With a gentle landing he might have had time to help the pilot, get the survival pack out. He watched the pilot carefully, noted everything he did, and realized how lucky he'd been. The pilot flared the plane out so that when it came down to the lake it seemed to be barely moving. He worked the wheel and rudder pedals to make it float down slowly and easily. Brian had more or less arrowed the plane into the water—through the trees and down—and it was a miracle that he hadn't been killed.

The answer to his problem had come to him while he slept.

It was simple.

The pilot was all business now, his hands working the controls, easing the throttle, settling the plane the last bit down to the lake.

But Derek turned and smiled at Brian. "Pretty, isn't it?"

And the lake *was* pretty. It was almost perfectly round, pushing out toward an egg shape slightly, but only slightly.

At the bottom edge of the lake and off to the right a short distance a river flowed south and east, and it was amazing to Brian how accurate the map had been.

They had gone over it on the dining room table, showing his mother where they would be, but looking down on it now, it seemed to be almost a model made of the map. The blue of the lake matched the blue of the water on the map and the river cutting southeast through the green forest looked just as it had on the map—delicate, winding.

Derek said something to the pilot—Brian couldn't hear over the sound of the engine—and the pilot nodded and banked the plane to the right, more toward the river, and put it softly onto the lake.

There was absolutely no wind, and the water was as smooth as a mirror. Brian watched out of his window as the float came down, saw its reflection in the water, closer, closer until it touched itself and skimmed across the flatness, settling more and more until the plane slowed nearly to a stop.

The pilot headed the plane toward a clearing to the right of where the river left the lake, nudging the throttle now and then to keep it moving on the floats until it at last slid through some green reeds and bumped the shoreline.

He cut the engine.

"We're here," Derek said, his voice loud in the sudden silence. "Let's get unloaded."

He turned and Brian could see that he was excited.

Like a kid, he thought. He's as excited as a kid. *I'm* the kid here, and I'm not excited. That's because he doesn't know. I know and he doesn't.

Derek climbed out onto the float—moving a little stiffly and Brian noted that he wasn't very athletic, seemed not to be too coordinated—and stepped ashore.

The pilot stayed in his seat and Brian moved the passenger seat forward and clambered out of the plane, stepped on the float and then to the dry grass.

Neat, he thought, neat and clean. The thought came into his mind that it was a beautiful day. The sun was out, there were small popcorn clouds moving across the sky, it was a soft summer afternoon.

Then, instantly—in just that part of a second—he changed. Completely. He became, suddenly, what he'd been before at the lake. Part of it, all of it; inside all of it so that every . . . single . . . little . . . *thing* became important.

He didn't just hear birds singing, not just a background sound of birds, but each bird. He listened to each bird. Located it, knew where it was by the sound, listened for the sound of alarm. He didn't just see clouds, but light clouds, scout clouds that came before the heavier clouds that could mean rain and maybe wind. The clouds were coming out of the northwest, and that meant that weather would come with them. Not could, but would. There would be rain. Tonight, late, there would be rain.

His eyes swept the clearing, then up the edge of the clearing, and in those two sweeps he knew—he *knew* the clearing and the woods. There was a stump there that probably held grubs; hardwood there for a bow, and willows there for arrows; a game trail, probably deer, moving off to the left meant other things, porcupines, raccoons, bear, wolves, moose, skunk would be moving on the trail and into the clearing. He flared his nostrils, smelled the air, pulled the air along the sides of his tongue in a hissing sound and tasted it, but there was nothing. Just summer smells. The tang of pines, soft air, some mustiness from rotting vegetation. No animals. At least, nothing fresh.

Derek had seen the change, was staring at him. "What happened?"

Brian shook his head. "Nothing."

"Yes—something did. You changed. Completely. You're not the same person."

Brian shrugged. "I was just . . . looking at things. Seeing them."

"Tell me," Derek said. He took a notebook out of his pocket. "Tell me everything you saw."

"Right now?"

"Yes."

"Shouldn't we let the pilot go first?"

Derek turned as if seeing the plane for the first time. "Oh, yes. I almost forgot. He has to get back. Let's unload, and then he can go and you can tell me—"

"No."

"What?"

Brian had made the decision just as he dozed off in the plane and it had settled into his mind while he slept. He knew it was the right thing to do. "We're not going to unload."

"What are you talking about?"

Brian looked at the lake, the clearing, the clouds. Seven, eight hours to rain. "I mean, if we unload all that gear—everything but the kitchen sink, like you said—this whole business will be ruined, wasted."

"I don't see what you mean—what happens if we have trouble?"

Brian nodded. "That's it exactly. We *have* trouble. That's what this is all about. You want to learn, but if you have all that backup, it's just more games. It's not real. You wouldn't have that if the situation were real, would you?"

"But we don't have to use it. We don't have to use any of it."

Brian smiled—a small, almost sad smile. "I promise you, absolutely promise you, that if that stuff is here you will use it and I will use it. By the third day, when the hunger really starts to work and the mosquitoes keep coming and coming and there isn't any food or a tent and we know it's just there, just in the bag—I guarantee you we will use it. We won't be able *not* to use it."

So much talk, Brian thought. Just jabber, jabber all the time. Like bluejays. We stand here and talk, and in seven, eight hours it will rain and we don't have shelter or dry wood or a fire going. Talk. "Leave it all in the plane. Leave it or I'm flying out of here right now. I know what's coming and I don't want to waste it."

"But we told your mother . . ."

Brian hesitated, then sighed. "I know. But the rule still holds. If we unload, I'm going home. Period. I'll take responsibility."

Derek studied him. "You mean it."

"Absolutely."

"How about a compromise?"

"What do you mean?"

"We keep the radio in case there's trouble—serious trouble. Then at least we can call for help."

Brian rubbed his neck, thinking. It wouldn't be the same. Even the radio would taint it. Still, he *had* told his mother not to worry and if he insisted on not using the radio, absolutely not using it . . .

"All right."

Derek nodded and stepped past him, balanced along the float and reached into the plane. He said something to the pilot, who nodded and looked at Brian through the windshield with a strange look, a studying look. Then he smiled and waved through the plastic and Brian nodded and waved in return.

Derek came back ashore with the radio—a small unit with a weatherproof seal and fresh nicad batteries. He also carried a small plastic briefcase.

"For my papers," he said. "I have to take notes, write things down."

Brian nodded, smiling inside. Derek sounded almost like Brian sounded when he was speaking to his mother or father and wanted to do something. Pleading. *For my papers . . .*

It was a strange feeling for Brian, the role reversal with an adult. He was in charge of an adult and he supposed in this situation it was the best way. But he was uncomfortable with it, the business of being in control over an adult—or anybody, for that matter.

The plane had to be turned. It was nosed into the reeds and the pilot opened the window and asked them to aim the plane around so it could taxi out and take off.

Derek and Brian worked it back and around, wading in the

water, pushing at the floats—the water felt warm to Brian, shore warm—and when they had it aimed well out, the pilot started the engine.

He taxied away without looking back and as soon as he was clear of the reeds he gunned the engine, increasing speed until the plane was roaring across the lake.

It bounced once, then again, and was airborne, climbed well over the trees at the end of the lake, circled and came back over them, the pilot wagging the wings as they watched, and then it was gone.

Gone.

"Well," Derek said. "Here we are. Alone."

Brian nodded. He felt a strange loss at watching the plane leave. An emptiness.

"What's next?" Derek asked. "How do we get the ball in play?"

Brian looked at him. A game, it's all a game. "A fire. We need a fire and shelter. Soon."

Derek looked at him, a question in his eyes.

Brian looked at the sky. "It's warm afternoon now, but with evening the mosquitoes will come and we need smoke to keep them away until coolness in the morning. And we need shelter because it's going to rain in about six and a half hours."

"Six and a half hours?"

"Sure. Can't you smell it?"

Derek took a breath through his nose, shook his head. "Nope. Not a thing."

"You will," Brian said. "You will. Now, let's . . . get the ball rolling." And he set off looking for a fire stone.

6

That first night Brian decided he was insane to have come back, insane to have agreed to do it, and insane for sending the plane away with all that wonderful equipment.

Especially the tent.

Brian had allowed them to have almost no survival gear. He decided that not all people put in this position would have a hatchet, so even that old friend was left at home.

He and Derek each had a knife, the kind that folds like a pocketknife, but is bigger and is worn on the belt in a leather case.

Other than that they had what was in their pockets.

Some change, a few dollars in paper money. Derek had a large nail clipper and some credit cards, Brian had pictures of his mother and Deborah in his wallet.

"That's it?" Derek had said early in the evening, while the

sun was still on them but low in the west, past the tops of the trees at the edge of the clearing.

"That's it." Brian had nodded.

"It's not much, is it?"

Brian had said nothing. The truth was, it *wasn't* much—especially for two people. They would need twice as much of everything. Twice as much food, a larger shelter—it changed things.

All Brian had needed to worry about before, during the Time, was himself. And that had been bad enough.

The thought of the second person, especially one as green as Derek, had not somehow hit him until just then, in late afternoon.

And then it didn't matter.

The plane was gone.

Things began to disintegrate fast after that.

It was one thing, Brian knew, to have a plan, to want to do things. It was something else to actually get them done.

Brian could not find a fire stone, so there was no fire.

Without fire there could be no smoke, and without smoke they had no protection against the mosquitoes.

They came with first dark and they were as bad as Brian had remembered. Thick clouds of them, whining, filling their eyes and ears and nostrils.

They had made a crude lean-to—Brian missed the overhanging rock with his shelter back inside a great deal. Clearly it would not stop the rain, though they had tried to make rough shingles of old pieces of half-rotted bark, yet it was a start.

But for some reason—some protective thought—they had crawled back into the lean-to when the mosquitoes first came.

As if, Brian thought, they could hide from the little monsters.

"God," Derek said in a whisper, a tight sound in the darkness back in the lean-to. "This is insane."

They were sitting with their jackets pulled over their heads, but due to Derek's size, when he pulled the jacket up, it pulled his shirt up from his waist and exposed a bit of skin there, and when the mosquitoes found that, he pulled the shirt down and it exposed his neck, and when he hunched to cover that, they could get his waist again, and in a small time he was jerking up and down like a yo-yo.

"You must settle," Brian told him. "In your mind. There are some fights you can't win, and I think this must be one of them. It will get worse and worse until after the middle of the night, when the coolness comes and the mosquitoes will stop. Or at least a lot of them will."

And just the words had helped, had calmed Derek and himself as well.

Dozing, listening to the whine of them around his head in the dark as they tried to find a way through the jacket, he thought, *it was the way.* It was the way of things here. The mosquitoes and the night and the coolness that he knew was coming were just the way of it—part of being here—and he thought he should tell Derek, but decided to keep his mouth shut.

Derek would find it for himself. Or he would not, just as Brian had found things out for himself.

Brian left the lean-to and went back outside. There might be part of a breeze later as the rain came and it would help.

There was a sliver of moon, which made enough light to see the lake well, the flat water with the beam of moonlight coming across it, and even with the mosquitoes still working at him he was amazed at the beauty.

There were night sounds—birds, flittering things he knew were bats. He also knew they were eating mosquitoes—he'd read about them in biology—and he thought, *get some, bats. Get some. Get all the mosquitoes there are.*

Something swam into the moonlight on the surface of the lake—either a muskrat or a beaver—and cut a *V* right up the path of the moon, seemed to be heading for the moon, into the moon itself.

Water made sound and he realized it was the river gurgling as it left the lake to his right. Not fast, and not wide—perhaps forty or fifty feet across—the river still seemed to possess force, strength as it ran.

Somehow the beauty overrode the mosquitoes. Brian was standing there, looking through the gap in his jacket—which was still pulled up over his head—when he heard Derek come up alongside him.

"It's incredible, isn't it?" Derek saw it as well, the beauty, and Brian was glad that he could see it, see not just the bad parts but the good as well.

"I had forgotten," Brian said. "I had dreams after I got out last time. Not all nightmares, but dreams. I would dream of this, of how pretty it was, how it could stop your breath with it, and then I would wake up in my room with the traffic sounds and the streetlights outside and I would feel bad—miss it. I would miss this."

"Except for the mosquitoes."

Brian smiled. "Well, yes, except for those."

But even as they talked, the night temperature started to drop and it was as if a switch went off. There were still some mosquitoes, but most of them left and the two of them were left standing in the moonlight.

"Incredible," Derek said. "They're just gone."

"Haven't you run into them before? You know, when you're doing the courses, and all that, for the government?"

Derek nodded. "Of course. Sort of. I haven't run the courses that much—just once to try to see what it was like and I pretty much failed it. They always have tents and repellent and gear with them. You know, to take the edge off." He laughed softly. "I'll change that the next time we have a meeting. It was wrong. Psychologically wrong. You were right to leave all that in the plane—absolutely right."

Later, when everything changed and he did not think there was hope, that statement was all that kept Brian going.

7

The rain came about eleven.

Derek had time for one quick joke.

"You said it would be six and a half hours—it's almost seven."

Then it hit them and there was nothing but water. The clouds had come quickly, covering the stars and moon in what seemed like minutes and then just opened up and dropped everything on them.

It wasn't just a rain. It was a roaring, ripping downpour of water that almost drove them into the ground.

They had moved back into the lean-to to try to get some rest since the mosquitoes partially lessened, but the temporary roof did nothing, absolutely nothing, to slow the water.

They were immediately soaked, then more soaked, sloppy with water.

They tried moving beneath some overhanging thick willows and birch near the edge of the lake, but the trees also did nothing to slow the downpour and finally they just sat, huddled beneath the willows, and took it.

I have, Brian thought, always been wet.

Always.

Even my soul is wet.

He felt the water running down his back. He judged it to be about the same rate as the faucet in his kitchen sink at home and that made him think of his mother.

Sitting at the table, the dining room table.

With a roof. He'd forgotten how nice a roof could be.

"This is crazy," he said aloud to Derek next to him, but the rain took the words away and he leaned against a birch and closed his eyes and, finally, took it.

I'm here, he thought, *to show Derek how I did it, how this can be done, for other people, and right now there is nothing to do but take it.*

And somehow the night passed.

Close to dawn the rain stopped and there was a softness after the rain, almost a warmth, and that brought the mosquitoes back for one more run. By the time the sun came up, full up over the lake and brought them warmth, Brian felt like he'd been hit by a truck while playing in a puddle.

He ached all over, and when he turned to see Derek—leaned back against a tree sideways, curled into a ball with his jacket still over his head—Brian laughed.

The sound awakened Derek, who was not really asleep, and he looked out of the jacket. "What's so funny?"

Brian shook his head. "I guess it's not funny, but you look so miserable—"

"You ought to see yourself." Derek grinned. "Kind of like a drowned rat."

"That's about how I feel."

They stood, and Brian moved down to the shore of the

lake. He stripped his clothes down to his shorts and wrung them out and hung them on some branches to dry.

This day, he thought, *this day we must find shelter and a fire stone and get a fire going and some food.*

Hunger was already there.

Not the kind that would come later, the cutting kind he remembered so well and that still made his mouth water when he walked past a grocery store or fast-food place.

But it was there.

"We have a problem," Derek said suddenly. He had moved down to the lake shore as well and had stripped down to hang his clothes to dry.

"That's for sure," Brian said. "We've definitely got a problem."

"No. Not what we're doing here. I mean, we have a problem with you."

"What do you mean?"

"You're so . . . so quiet. I mean, I see you looking at things and thinking, but I don't know what you're thinking about or what you're working out. I have to know all this to write about it, to tell people what to do."

Brian nodded. "I understand. It's just that the last time I did this I was alone."

I would have killed, Brian thought suddenly, for someone to talk to, someone to share it with, someone to hear me; and now that I have someone, I don't talk.

"It's kind of strange having someone here with me."

Derek nodded. "That's what I mean. You have to tell me everything, externalize it all for me, so I can write it."

Derek moved back to the lean-to, where he'd left the radio and his weatherproof briefcase. Inside the briefcase he had notebooks, each one in a plastic bag, and he took one out now with a pencil and began to write carefully. When he'd written something he looked up at Brian, waiting. "All right. I'm ready."

Externalize, Brian thought. How do you externalize?

"Well, I'm thinking now that we should make sure we get a shelter today and then get a fire today and get some food today. . . ."

I sound like a catalog, he thought, *like I'm reading a telephone book.*

But Derek nodded and started writing and Brian thought of what he really wanted to say.

We should grab the radio and call for the plane and go home and eat a hamburger and a malt, maybe eight or ten Cokes, a steak, some roasts and pork chops. . . .

He shook his head.

"There," Derek said. "What were you thinking there?"

Brian stared at him, then shook his head. "You don't want to know. Just junk."

He walked away into the day. It was enough. Enough of talk. Enough of externalizing. Another night like last night would kill him.

He left his clothes to dry, but wore his tennis shoes and noticed that Derek did the same thing—although he carried the notebook as well—and Brian set off along the lakeshore to the left.

Rule one, he thought, don't leave the lakeshore or you'll get lost. Then he remembered Derek and said it aloud.

"Thank you," Derek said, rather properly. Standing in his underwear holding the notebook he looked like somebody out of an old, funny movie and Brian had trouble keeping a straight face. "That's exactly what I meant by externalizing."

"We're looking for a fire stone, a shelter, and food—all at once. Always, always you look for food. There, up along the edge of the clearing—you see those stumps?"

Derek nodded.

"Those will be a good bet for grubworms later."

"Grubworms?"

"Sure. Bears eat them—love to eat them. I can't eat them yet, but by about the third day if we don't find something else or get some fish they'll probably be looking pretty good."

"Grubworms?"

Brian smiled. "I thought you did this survival thing once before."

"Oh, we ate lizards and snakes and stuff like that—they always have the course in the desert. Or did until now. I think it will change. And you always read about people eating ants and grasshoppers, but I never ate a grubworm."

"You don't chew them," Brian said. "I think that would be too much. Just to chew one up, guts and all. They're too soft and, well, just too soft. But if you wrap them in leaves and swallow them whole . . ."

"Right," Derek nodded and wrote in the notebook. "Grubworms."

Brian stopped and turned to Derek. "Food is everything."

"What do you mean?"

"Just that. Out here, in nature, in the world, food is everything. All the other parts of what we are, what everything is, don't matter without food. I read somewhere that all of what man is, everything man has always been or will be, all the thoughts and dreams and sex and hate and every little and big thing is dependent on six inches of topsoil and rain when you need it to make a crop grow—food."

"You sound like you've thought this out."

"That's *all* I did—think of food. You watch other animals, birds, fish, even down to ants—they spend all their time working at food. Getting something to eat. That's what nature is, really—getting food. And when you're out here, having to live, you look for food. Food first. Food. *Food.*"

They moved through the day that way. During midmorning they found some raspberries growing in a brushpile. It was not a thick stand—it would maybe have been enough for one person, but with two it was skimpy—still, there were some and they worked through the brush in their underwear, eating every berry they could find.

They also found some chokecherries—what Brian had called gut cherries—but Brian shook his head. "Later, if we have to, and then in small amounts."

Brian kept moving along the lake, waiting, walking, and waiting, and he realized at length what he was waiting for—what was in the back of his mind.

Luck.

You move and you watch and you work hard and you just keep doing that until luck comes. If it's bad luck you ride it out and if it comes the other way and you have good luck you're ready for it.

They had good luck in the middle of the afternoon. And as so often seems to happen, the good luck came about because of bad luck.

8

Brian had moved out ahead, down and to the right of Derek, and was working closer to the edge of the lake. Derek worked up and away from the lake, looking for more berries as they moved.

"Stay in sight of me," Brian had told him. "Don't get away from the lake so far that you can't see, and if you run into a bear don't look into his eyes."

"Bear?"

"They hunt for food, too, and eat berries. We'll probably see one. Just back away and don't look at them—I read that it's a threat when you do that."

"Bear?"

Brian was glad to see that his warning had been taken and Derek was always within sight.

Here the land rose as they approached the northern end of the lake. It came up in a low roll that made a sizable hill next to the lake. Because of this rise and the freezing and thawing of the lake, the movement of the ice each winter, the land had been cut away, washed still further away by heavy rains —Brian could see the work of last night's rain—and all this chewing at the side of the hill had left something close to a small cliff.

It wasn't terribly high—thirty feet or so—but it was steep and very unstable, the edge loose and soft from the rain.

Brian had moved close to the edge. Down below he could see into the green water of the lake and there were fish moving and the sight made him realize how hungry he was becoming. It had been over a day now—they had eaten normally the day before when they flew to the lake—and the hunger was becoming demanding.

He turned to see Derek, who was coming up the back of the hill. "See the fish—"

Brian had come too close to the soft soil at the edge, and before he could finish the sentence, the bank let go.

He dropped like an anvil, his finger still pointing at the fish. Halfway down the face of the cut there was a small outcropping of soil and rocks mixed, held in place because it was made of clay and chalk bound together, and Brian hit this mound on his stomach. Hard.

"Ooomph!" He heard himself sound like the air going out of a tire, then he bounced up and sideways and continued on down to the bottom in a shower of mud and rocks, to where a small gravel beach led into the lake.

I don't think I'll move, he thought, lying flat on his face. *Ever again.*

Derek was by his side in moments, frowning in worry. "Are you hurt?"

I wonder why people ask that, Brian thought. *Did he think I could do this and* not *hurt?*

But he shook his head. "No. At least I don't think so. . . ."

He rose, or put his hands down to push himself up, and as he made the move he noticed the rocks around him on the beach. Most of them were round and smooth, rubbled by wind and water and weather and time, but mixed in with them were black, hardened shards.

Where he'd fallen there were fresh ones, not weathered, and he saw that they had come from the bank where he had bounced.

"Look," Brian held up one of the black stones. It was chipped and layered. "I think it might be the same kind of stone I used to make fire with the hatchet."

"Flint," Derek said. "I think it is."

Brian took out his knife, opened it and locked the blade, and struck the back of the hard steel against the sharp edge of the flint. Three, four times he hit and finally there were sparks.

He looked up, smiling. "No more mosquitoes."

He took two of the larger black stones and they went to find a campsite, and here, too, there was the waiting for luck.

They walked nearly halfway around the lake, looking always as well for food. As they worked past the northern end of the lake they came on low brush filled with small nuts. These he knew were hazelnuts, and they stopped to pick and eat some. They were ripe, or very close, just shy of being dry, and the worms and squirrels had been at them, but they still found enough to cut the edge off their hunger. They used rocks to smash them and spent over an hour bashing rocks and nibbling at the small chunks of nutmeat, which tasted almost sweet.

It was then approaching evening and Brian knew they would need a shelter of some kind and a fire, before dark and the evening horde of insects found them.

Then, coming out of a stand of thick willows, they found it.

In some ancient time, an enormous tree had fallen in a giant wind. The tree had been growing on the side of a small hill, which was made on a rocky shelf. As the tree went over it pulled earth, balled in its roots, with it, and made a large hole back in, under the shelf of rocks.

Time had done the rest. The tree was long rotted and gone to worms, the soil had filtered somewhat back into the hole and taken grass seeds, and what was left was a large depression in the side of the hill with an overhanging shelf of rock. On each side of the depression there were large trees—white pines that went towering up and shaded the whole place to make it feel like a quiet garden.

It was not perfect, not as nice as Brian had had on the *L*-shaped lake. But it was good enough, far better than nothing, and to cap it off, there was a small spring of water to the side of the overhang, where a fissure of rock let water work out in a trickle that made its way down to the lake.

"Home," Brian said.

Derek looked at the depression. "It looks like a hole—what do we do to make it livable?"

"Beds and a fire. You use pine boughs to make the beds." He showed Derek how to cut the boughs and stick them point down to make a soft bed. "You do that and I'll work on a fire."

"I need to watch you do that," Derek said. "So I can write about it."

Brian nodded and set out to find what he needed.

He would never forget the first fire, what it had meant to him—as important as it must have been to early man—and he approached making a fire now almost as a religious experience.

You could not hurry it, he knew. Fire would come only

when it wanted to come, and only when there was a good bed for it, a home for it.

He found some birches near the shoreline and shredded dry birch bark with his fingernails until it was like hair. He kept adding to this until he had a ball of fluff three inches in diameter.

To this he added some pulverized, dried grass, worked almost into flour, and when it was all together, he gently used his finger to make a hole in the middle.

A home for the fire, he thought. A place for it to live.

Derek had watched all of this with intense interest, writing in his notebook from time to time, underlining things, nodding.

Brian set aside the tinder and found some dry pine twigs, as small as matches. When he had a good pile of these, broken and lined up for use, he searched for slightly larger dry wood and still larger until he had a pile as high as his knees.

In all of this he was silent, thinking only of the fire, but he turned to Derek now. "You can't have too much wood. Ever. And you should always have dried wood stashed back in some safe place, along with tinder. . . ." He paused, thinking, remembering.

"What is it?" Derek asked.

"Fire. It's so . . . so alive. Such an important thing to us. Back there in the world we don't know that. But when I got home last time I tried to read about what it was like, you know, before we got everything we have now. In colonial times they kept people awake just to watch the fires, and in ancient times the most important person in the tribe was called the fire watcher."

Derek wrote it down and Brian smiled. Something about Derek walking around all day looking for berries and nuts, carrying a briefcase like a business executive, seemed ridiculous. But he meant what he was doing and Brian liked him more and more all the time. When he'd fallen and Derek had kneeled next to him, he had been genuinely worried.

Fire.

There was a lowering of light now and evening would not be long, accompanied by the waiting bugs.

He and Derek made a small fire pit in front of the overhang. Then Brian put the tinder on the ground in the pit so that the flame cup was aimed upward.

Over this he held the piece of flint.

He struck it with the knife and nothing came.

Naturally, he thought. If it were easy, everybody would want to do this.

He hit again and again and finally the sparks came. Now he slammed the stone with the back of the knife blade with renewed force, again and again until a small shower of sparks fell into the cup.

Quickly he raised the tinder in his hand, blowing gently, softly on the sparks, watching as they became glowing holes in the tinder and the holes grew, became red, turned to coals and finally, blowing as he put it back on the ground, smoke curling up into his eyes, there came the tiny flicker of new flame.

Hello, he thought—*hello, flame.* Fire.

He fed small twigs to the flame, crossing them and recrossing them until the fire was full, healthy. Then he added larger sticks and still larger until they filled the pit and there was the crackling sound of a full fire.

Brian settled back on his haunches and smiled; looked up at Derek, who was also smiling.

Brian gestured around with his hand. "No more mosquitoes—the smoke keeps them away. It doesn't even take much, just a little blowing around. But we need more wood."

They took the next hour to gather wood, stacking it until they had a large pile to the side of the camp, and Derek used the time to cut pine boughs for beds as well. When it was late, and they finally lay back to rest, they had done much to make the overhang a home.

Brian went to sleep on his side. The last thing he heard before he dozed was the sound of a wolf. He heard Derek rise.

"It's a wolf," Brian said. "Far away, just singing. Besides, wolves don't bother you. You can go back to sleep."

And Derek did, rolling over, his breathing even, and Brian let sleep come again.

9

Brian stood away from the fish trap and shook his head.

Nothing was the same, really.

It was a beautiful day, with the mid-afternoon sun shining down on them, and he thought of what the problem could be, what was wrong.

It had somehow turned into one big happy camping trip.

We might as well have a cooler full of soft drinks and sandwiches, Brian thought.

They'd been at the lake three days, but it looked like they'd been there a year. The camp was squared away and neat. Derek had called in on the radio and told the world they were all right, telling them to pass the information on to Brian's parents—Brian thought his mother might worry if she knew about them sending the gear back. Then they had enhanced the beds and made them deep and soft with more boughs, there was enough firewood for a month, and they had made birch-bark containers to hold extra hazelnuts and berries.

They'd found blueberries and raspberries and plums. On this side of the lake the forest was more open and the plums and nuts and berries seemed to thrive in the light and heat.

Wild plums. They were a little green, but even so, Brian couldn't believe how sweet and rich they were—like small, domestic plums, with a little more tang to them.

Brian had made a bow, used a strip from his belt for a string, and had shown Derek how to shoot fish, then how to use the guts from one fish to bait the others into a trap made of stones; and they soon had more fish than they needed. Brian found a clam bed and they had actually eaten one meal—clams steamed around the fire, nuts, and berries—that left them full.

Full.

Plus, they had more clams stored and plenty of fish left in the trap and knew the locations of several ruffed grouse. There were rabbits and squirrels all over the place, and if they had to they could make it a year or two, and it felt wrong.

All wrong.

He shook his head again and moved back by the fire pit. Derek was sitting on his bed by the fire, feeding an occasional stick to the fire to keep it going, writing in his notebook. He looked up as Brian walked into the shelter, and saw him shaking his head.

"What's the matter?"

Brian shrugged. "I don't know—it's just wrong, I think."

"What do you mean—wrong?"

Brian looked around at the shelter, the comfort, the food, the fire, the lake. "All this. We're so . . . so ready. So calm. It doesn't work, somehow. None of it works."

"I still don't know for sure what you're talking about. We've done it. In four days you've shown me how to live in the wilderness with nothing but a knife. I've got tons of notes to take back and teach from—I think you're wrong."

"But this isn't how it works," Brian said. "It isn't this smooth and easy. You don't just fly in and get set on a perfect lake and have all the food you want and have it all come this easy. It isn't real."

Derek leaned back, put his hands in back of his head, and looked at Brian.

"There's not a thing to make it rough . . . nothing wrong. In a real situation, like when I was here before, there were things wrong—going wrong. The plane didn't land and set me on the shore. It crashed. A man was dead. I was hurt. I didn't know anything. Nothing at all. I was, maybe, close to death and now we're out here going la-de-da, I've got a fish; la-de-da, there are some more berries."

"Tension." Derek said. "It lacks tension."

Brian nodded. "Maybe—but that's not all. I don't think you can *teach* what you want to teach."

"But they do—they teach survival."

"No. I think they tell people what to do and maybe you can tell them some of what we do. But that doesn't teach them *how* to live, *how* to do it, does it? You'd have to bring each person here and drop them in the lake and let them swim out and drag up the shore and try to live, to really *teach* them how to do it. Every single one."

"But that's impossible."

Brian nodded. "I know. But I don't think it will work unless you do it that way. You can tell, but you can't really teach."

"Tension," Derek said again, leaning forward and writing

in his notebook again. "You need the tension created by the emergency."

And they settled in for the rest of the day and that night, and later Brian would remember what they had said—how it needed tension—and wish he had not thought it at all.

10

Brian awakened suddenly, and listened, and smelled.

For a moment he could not tell what had brought him up from sleep. They had banked the fire well and the coals would last until morning. It was still warm and red, giving off a little smoke. There were no bugs, the night cool wasn't too cold, no animals prowled, and he could find nothing wrong and was closing his eyes to sleep again when he heard it.

The far-off sound of thunder. Not loud; low and rumbling. He could smell rain coming, but that should pose no problem. The storms and the wind came from the north-northwest and they had the hill in back to protect them. With the overhang facing south and being on the side of the hill, the rain wouldn't bother them. In fact, they'd had an evening of soft rain and nothing had come in the shelter—not a drop.

And with the storm blowing any rain away from the opening, they should stay dry and safe.

Brian put a couple of pieces of wood on the fire to make sure it kept going, added a handful of green leaves to make smoke and keep the mosquitoes down, checked to see that Derek was still sleeping, and lay back on his bed.

Maybe the storm wouldn't even hit them. He remembered the tornado that had caught him before and decided he wouldn't worry. The odds against getting hit twice by anything as wild as a tornado were huge, and there was nothing they could do anyway, except just hope that it would miss them. He remembered the sound the tornado had made—the wild roaring—and the storm it had come from, and this was different.

A summer rainstorm with soft thunder—it didn't seem anything to worry about and certainly nothing to keep him awake. He went back to sleep, slipping into a light doze.

Things moved in and out—he dreamed that he was talking to Derek, saying in the dream that he thought they should use the radio to call the plane and cancel the rest of the "operation," as Derek kept calling it in the dream, because it didn't seem to prove anything.

He was awakened by an explosion.

It seemed to come from inside his skull, inside his thinking, inside the dream: a sharp crack, so loud that he snapped awake, rolled over, and was on his feet, moving to the back of the shelter without thinking, without knowing he was moving.

It was thunder.

But not like he'd heard before, not like he'd ever heard. It was around them, exploding around them, the lightning cracking around the shelter, so close it seemed to Brian that it came from inside him.

"What—"

He knew that he opened his mouth, that he made sound, but he could hear nothing except the *whack-crack* of the thunder, see nothing but images frozen in the split-instants of brilliance from the lightning.

Like a camera taking pictures by a strobe light, things would seem frozen in time, caught and frozen, and then there would be another flash and things would be different.

Derek was moving.

In one flash he was still on his bed, but raised, his jacket falling away from where he'd had it as a blanket, as he rose.

Darkness.

Then the next flash of light and he was on his knees.

Darkness.

Then he was leaning forward and his hand was out, reaching for his briefcase and radio next to the bed, one finger out, his face concentrating; and Brian thought, no, don't reach, stay low; and he might have yelled it, screamed it, but it didn't matter. No sound could be loud enough to get over the thunder.

There was a slashing, new, impossibly loud crack as lightning seemed to hit the shelter itself and Brian saw the top of the pine next to the opening suddenly explode and felt/saw the bolt come roaring down the tree, burning and splitting and splintering the wood and bark, and he saw it hit Derek.

Camera image.

Some *thing,* some blueness of heat and light and raw power seemed to jump from the tree to the briefcase and radio and enter Derek's hand. All in the same part of a second it hit him and his back arched, snapped him erect, and then it seemed to fill the whole shelter and slammed into Brian as well.

He saw the blueness, almost a ball of energy, the crack/flash of color that came from inside his mind, inside his life, and then he was back and down and saw nothing more.

11

Before his eyes opened there was light through the eyelids, bright light, but they didn't want to open and focus. He tasted things, smelled things. Something was burned, there was the stink of something burned. Hair. Burned hair.

It smelled awful.

He opened his eyes wide, blinked, forced them to work and saw that he was on his back, looking at the stone-layered ceiling of the overhang.

It was daylight, broad daylight, and he wondered why it was that he would be lying on his back on the dirt, looking at the ceiling in the middle of the day.

Then he remembered.

Parts of it: the sound, the light, the thunder, and the slamming and cracking of it; and he was afraid. He did not know what he was afraid of at first, he was just afraid, and then, finally, he remembered Derek.

It had hit him.

He had seen it hit Derek.

He rolled on his side. His body felt stiff, mashed into the ground, and the sudden movement made his vision blur.

There.

He saw Derek—or the form of Derek. He was facedown on his bed, his right hand out, his left arm back and down his side. Blurred, he was all blurred and asleep—how could he be all blurred? Brian shook his head, tried to focus.

Derek was still asleep. How strange, Brian thought—how strange that Derek should still be asleep in the bright daylight, and he knew then that Derek was not sleeping, but did not want to think of the other thing.

Let's reason it out, he thought, his mind as blurred as his vision. Reason it all out. Derek was reaching for the radio and briefcase and the lightning hit the tree next to the shelter and came down the tree and across the air and into Derek and he fell. . . .

No.

He was still asleep.

He wasn't that other thing. Not that other word.

But Brian's eyes began to clear then and saw that Derek was lying with his head to the side and that it was facing Brian and the eyes weren't closed.

They were open.

He was on his side not moving and his eyes were open and Brian thought how strange it was that he would sleep that way—mashed on his stomach.

He knew Derek wasn't sleeping.

He knew.

"No. . . ."

He couldn't be. Couldn't be . . . dead. Not Derek.

Finally, he accepted it.

Brian rose to his hands and knees, stiff and with great slowness, and crawled across the floor of the shelter to where Derek lay.

The large man lay on his stomach as he'd dropped, his head turned to the left. The eyes were not fully open, but partially lidded, and the pupils stared blankly, unfocused toward the back of the shelter.

Brian touched his cheek. He remembered how when the pilot had his heart attack he had felt cool—the dead skin had felt cool.

Derek's skin did not have the coolness, it felt warm; and Brian kneeled next to him and saw that he was breathing.

Tiny little breaths, his chest barely rising and falling, but he was breathing, the air going in and out, and he was not the other word—not dead—and Brian leaned over him.

"Derek?"

There was no answer, no indication that Derek had heard him.

"Derek. Can you hear anything I'm saying?"

Still no sign, no movement.

So, Brian thought—so he's what? He's knocked out. He got hit and he's knocked out and if I wait and make him comfortable he'll come out of it.

That was it. Just knocked out.

Derek's head looked twisted at an uncomfortable angle and Brian moved Derek's body onto its side and set his head—the neck felt rubbery and loose—on his rolled-up jacket for a pillow. As he did he saw the briefcase and radio.

The radio.

There it was, right there on the briefcase; and if there was ever a need for it, it was now.

He picked it up, turned the switch on.

"Katie One, this is Katie Two, over."

His mother's name. It was a small thing, a way to include his mother. They used her name as the call sign and Derek had shown Brian how to use the radio, the correct procedure in case of an emergency.

Like now.

"Katie One, this is Katie Two, over."

Nothing. He turned the squelch control down and listened for the hiss of static, but there was nothing. Not even noise.

Again.

"Katie One, this is Katie Two, over."

Dead air. He saw, then, that next to where the antenna came out of the case, there was a small discolored spot on the plastic. It was a burn mark. The radio was made to be used outdoors, tough, with a weatherproof case around it, and when he opened the outside case he saw that the lightning had hit the radio as well as Derek and him.

There was a jagged line burned in the plastic on the back and even without opening the case and seeing the inside he knew the radio was blown.

What to do? Think. He couldn't think right.

He put the radio down and turned back to Derek. There was no change at all—no movement except for the short rise and fall of his chest with his breathing. The eyes were still partially opened, as they had been.

Think.

What did he know that could help?

Lightning had hit the tree next to the overhang, come down the side—he saw where the pine bark was burned and literally blown from the tree—and then must have come out on a root or jumped away from the tree somehow.

No, that wasn't right. He'd read somewhere that lightning struck *up,* not down—moved from the ground up.

Somehow it had come from the ground, through Derek and the radio and him to the tree, and then up, except that it seemed to come down and Derek shouldn't have reached out, shouldn't have risen. . . .

He shook his head. Stupid. None of that mattered.

Electrical shock. What did you do when there was electrical shock?

C.P.R.

To get them breathing again, you had to give them C.P.R. —except that Derek was breathing already.

Heart. He should check the heart.

He put his fingers on Derek's wrist, but couldn't find the pulse—but when he checked his own he couldn't find that either. He put his ear to Derek's chest and heard the heart thumping. He tried to time it, but couldn't transpose the number of beats per minute measured on his digital watch into a pulse rate because he couldn't think.

Think.

The lightning came, took the tree, then Derek, the radio, him—and they were all knocked down and out.

There it was—maybe Derek was just knocked out and would come to in a little while.

Somehow he knew that wasn't true. Something in the way Derek looked made the condition look like more than just being knocked out. Yet Brian wanted it to be, wanted it to be so much that he forced himself to believe it.

Derek was breathing evenly—short breaths, but even—and his heart was beating regularly.

He was just knocked out.

Brian would make him comfortable and then wait next to him. Wait for him to come to.

He would wait.

12

The rest of that day and through the night, he kneeled next to Derek.

Waiting.

He only moved to get a drink and eat some berries and go to the bathroom, the rest of the time he kneeled next to Derek, putting a piece of wood on the fire now and then to keep it going, waiting. Waiting.

And he knew.

He knew that Derek was not just unconscious, was more seriously hurt than that, and still he did not know what to do.

Or if he could do anything.

The radio was gone. They had made a schedule that said they would check in once a week or so—it was very loose—and that they would call if there was an emergency. Derek had just done the weekly check-in the afternoon before, so they wouldn't think it odd that there were no calls. The bush-plane headquarters said they would keep their radio on around the clock, but not necessarily manned all the time, so even if he had a radio, Brian might not be able to get them right away. Of course, he could call any other airplane and report the emergency.

If he had a radio.

So he could not call for help, and they would not worry for another week or so, when Derek did not call in. There they were, where they sat.

Derek was down, unconscious.

In a coma.

There. *That* word came. He had been afraid of the word *death* before and now this word, *coma.* He'd have to stop that, have to face things better than he was facing them. He knew almost nothing of medical terms or what happened to people with severe shock, and knew less than nothing about comas.

He'd seen movies about people in comas for months and months or years and years and then they would suddenly snap out of it and wonder how long they'd been asleep.

In the night, next to Derek, he tried to will him awake. *Snap awake now and ask how long you've been sleeping. Now. And we'll laugh and talk about how close the lightning came.*

But it did not work.

Derek did not awaken, made no change of any kind. Somewhere just before dawn, when the first light of false dawn was making the western side of the lake come into view, Brian finally accepted it.

Derek was in a coma and was apparently not going to snap out of it. At least not soon.

That left everything, everything on Brian, and for a moment he felt a touch of anger and resentment.

The woods.

The damn woods.

Last time he'd almost died, would have died, except for luck, and now this—this again. All this dumped on him just because he tried to do the right thing, and he didn't even want to do it. Anyway, Derek was so dumb that he raised up and reached out when he should have stayed low and . . . and . . . and. . . .

Listen to me, he thought. *If I were talking out loud, I'd be whining.*

Derek gets hit and I act like I'm the one getting messed up.

It was this way, he thought. Derek was unconscious and it seemed to be a coma—or something like a coma.

He did not seem to be coming out of it.

The radio did not work and Brian could not call for help.

So, then what?

They might come looking in a week or ten days. Could he stay here with Derek for a week or ten days and wait for them?

Could he *not* stay? What choices did he have?

If he stayed and Derek didn't regain consciousness, how long would he . . . last? If he didn't get food and water, could he stay alive?

They never talked about that in movies or on television. They never said what they did with people in a coma. Fed them through tubes, probably.

But he couldn't do that.

He had to try to put food and water down Derek's throat, and if he did that he might choke him and kill him.

So he couldn't really do that, either.

"So, then," he said aloud, speaking to and not to Derek at the same time. "What can I do?"

He had kneeled next to Derek almost all night, and when

he tried to stand, his knees almost buckled. He rolled sideways and flexed his legs, and while he was rolled to the side he smelled it.

Oh, yes—I'd forgotten that kind of thing—the bathroom. Derek would, of course, have to go to the bathroom—his body functions would keep going. Or would they? Yes, apparently they would.

There was that too. To take care of Derek, truly take care of him—he'd never had to do anything like it before, take care of someone.

Himself, sure, but he'd never been really responsible for some other person, and he wondered what to do—what a person did.

The anger had passed, but he felt immense frustration at his helplessness.

It had to be done. He had to clean Derek, take care of him, take care of another human being. Look at it that way, he thought—not Derek, but another person. He had to clean this helpless person—if he kept it detached, maybe he could do it.

Why would it be so hard anyway?

He unfastened Derek's pants and the smell grew stronger.

"Oh, God."

He fought the nausea down, controlled it, turned Derek over and held his breath and used grass to clean him. Then he pulled the pants up and put him on his side again.

Parents—how did parents do it? It was horrible—how could they do it? He used sticks to carry it and the grass to the hole they had dug for a bathroom and covered it with dirt, then went down to the lake and washed his hands again and again until he could hold them to his face and not smell anything. When they were clean and he could breathe normally without choking, he went back to Derek.

Comfort—he could do what he could to make Derek more

comfortable. Brian moved him and rearranged the pine boughs to make a softer bed.

Then he pulled Derek onto his back on the new boughs, but was alarmed when Derek seemed to begin to choke or breathe strangely, and he put him back on his side.

So, nothing.

Nothing he could do, not really.

It was full light now, warm, with the sun drying the rain off the grass. A warm summer morning with birds singing, Brian thought, looking across the mirrored surface of the lake —a beautiful summer morning with birds singing and fish jumping on the lake and everything perfect, except for this one thing. This one little thing.

Derek was in a coma.

13

Somewhere, Brian thought, somewhere he'd heard something about comas. He must have. Something more than he could remember. But it had to be in his mind, in his thinking, and if it was there he must be able to get it out.

He spent the morning trying to remember what he knew, but nothing came.

It was like being asleep, except that you didn't wake up, he thought. Everything kept working, but you couldn't eat or drink.

He had been moving from the lake to the shelter with a birch-bark cone full of water when it hit him.

They could wait all week, wait nine or ten days for the plane to come—or he could. He knew that people had gone that long without food. Derek would lose some weight, but he wouldn't starve to death in that time.

But Brian was sure Derek could not go that long without water. Two, three days, maybe four, then he would be in trouble. Somewhere he'd heard or read or seen that the human body couldn't go that long without water.

And it had already been one day, going on two days.

He could try getting Derek to drink. If he could get water in him he would last. His breathing had steadied still more and his heart rate was close to normal. Brian had finally settled enough to measure it and calculate that it was running about sixty-five beats per minute. He remembered something about the rate supposing to be seventy-two, so Derek was low, but it was still working all right.

Brian made a small spoonlike holder out of birch bark. With this he dipped water from the cone, which he had propped next to Derek's head, and he put a small bit of water into the unconscious man's mouth.

The effect was immediate and explosive.

"Charrsst!"

Derek choked instantly, and reflex action took over and he coughed, spraying water and spit in Brian's face. The choking continued and Brian frantically pulled Derek's head over to the side, held his face down and pounded on his back—all he knew to do.

It seemed to last forever and Brian was terrified that he had killed Derek. One mistake, one thing wrong, and he was choking to death.

But finally the water cleared from Derek's throat and the coughing stopped, though his breathing was still ragged.

"So, you can't drink." Brian settled Derek's head back onto the rolled-up jacket. "That doesn't make all this any easier."

At first he felt strange, talking to Derek when there was no indication that he could be heard. Then he remembered his mother reading a story in a paper and telling him about a girl that had been in a coma for months—please, he thought, dear

God, don't let Derek be under that long—and when she recovered she said that while she was in the coma she could hear people talking. She could hear and understand, but could not answer, and he thought Derek might be the same.

"Derek?" He leaned close to Derek's face. "Can you hear me?"

There was no sign.

"Can you move your eyelids? If you hear me, move your eyelids."

Nothing. The eyes were half open, filled with tears that came constantly. Apparently the body was trying to keep them from drying out, because Derek could not blink.

He sat up, then stood and looked at the sky. *I can't do this,* he' thought. *I can't do this alone. I just can't. . . .*

He looked down at Derek again, shook his head. "I don't know what to do."

And he realized then that he was wrong—it wasn't like last time. He wasn't alone.

There was Derek. Maybe if he talked to him, spoke aloud to him—maybe it might help.

"Here it is," Brian said, squatting again, moving a stick in the dirt. "There's no way anybody will come for at least a week, and maybe longer. Maybe ten days. I don't think you can . . . I don't think it would be good to go that long without water. I can't get you to drink because I think you'll choke. So."

"So." He repeated, shrugging, drawing a big zero in the dirt. "I don't know what to do."

He threw the stick down in exasperation. It hit the ground harder than he meant, then bounced and skipped into Derek's briefcase.

Brian saw it as if for the first time. He'd forgotten about it in the crisis and went to it. "What have you got in here?"

It was not locked and he opened it with the two sliding thumb releases on either end of the handle edge.

Inside, there were spiral notebooks. They weren't anything special—the kind with ruled lines and the twisted wire holding the edge—and each of them was numbered.

He opened number one.

"Arrived," he read aloud. "Brian demanded that we leave all the gear in the plane or it would ruin the whole experiment."

Oh, yes, Brian thought—*I did that. Oh, God, I did that, didn't I? I stuck my little foot down and dug in and got stubborn and set all this up. What was there? Food and shelter and a gun and all the things I didn't think we'd need that would make this easier.*

"I admire his ethics." He finished reading the first day. He put the notebook down. "You do, eh? Admire me—the guy who made us lose all that gear?"

He felt like he was prying and decided not to read any more of the notebooks. He started to close the briefcase and saw that there was a folding accordion-style section that collapsed back into the lid.

There was something in the section and he pulled out a folded paper. When he opened it he saw that it was the map.

The same map they had looked at with Brian's mother. He saw the lake, saw where they had circled it with her, showing where they would be, how . . . how *located* it looked. How easy to see and find and locate.

Derek had had two copies of the map and he'd left one with Brian's mother. "So you can always tell right where we are."

Brian remembered sitting there, his mother smiling. All her questions answered, all her doubts gone.

And now look at them.

Derek had brought the other map and kept it when Brian

dug his heels in and told him to send everything but the radio back and in some relief Brian had spread the map gratefully on the back of the briefcase—thinking it would help—but now he shook his head and started to fold it. What difference did it make if he knew where they were? It wouldn't help them.

Then he looked at the lake again, saw how it lay in the wide, flat greenness—how there were many lakes around it.

And he saw the river.

14

He had noticed it before, of course—when they went over the map in his house and when they had first landed. But in the largeness of the country shown on the map, the massive forest the map showed, the river was a small thing, and he had negated it.

It wound out the bottom of the lake, the southern end, and headed southeast down into the lakes below and was lost, and he had not followed it except to note the name.

The Necktie River.

"Isn't that a funny name," his mother had said, and Derek had laughed.

"There are lakes named Eunice, or Bootsock—there are so many lakes and rivers, the original mapmakers just made up names as they went. The person drawing the map was probably wearing a tie and thought it would make a good name. Many of them aren't named at all—just numbered."

The Necktie River, Brian saw, led south and down and drew his eyes away from the lake.

The map was laid out in square five-thousand-meter grids—five-kilometer squares—and he saw that in some places the river wound back almost on itself inside the same five thousand square meters. But in other places it ran straight for a considerable distance and he followed it, through smaller lakes and what he thought must be swamps, through the darker green portions that meant heavier forest.

It kept going south to the edge of the map, where it was folded, and he unfolded the next section and spread it in the sun. He did not know why the river drew him, pulled at him.

Then, halfway through the second page, he saw it. The river had grown all along, gotten wider so that it made a respectable blue cut across the map and where it made a large bend, cutting back nearly straight east, there was a small circle drawn and the words:

Brannock Trading Post.

Leading away from Brannock's Post there was a double line heading down and to the southwest. When he found the symbol for the double line on the map's legend he saw that it stood for an improved gravel road.

There would be people there.

Right there, on the map, at Brannock's Trading Post there would be people. They wouldn't have a road or name the place or make it a dot on the map unless there were people there. A trading post would have people.

Which, Brian thought, doesn't mean a thing.

He wasn't at Brannock's Trading Post. He was here.

Yet he couldn't take his eyes off the spot on the map. It was there, on the same map—just there. And he refolded the map so it would show the lake where they were and the trading post at the same time. He used his fingers to make a divider and measured it straight down, but it didn't mean anything.

Then he remembered that the grids stood for five kilometers each, and when he counted the numbers of grids between the lake and Brannock's he came up with about sixteen squares.

"So how far is that?" he said to Derek. "Five times sixteen —maybe eighty, eighty-five kilometers."

But that was straight—in a straight line southeast.

The river was nowhere near straight, looping back and forth and actually flowing slightly north back along itself at one point.

He started counting, measuring the river as it turned through each five-kilometer square, marking each ten kilometers in the dirt with a line through it, then the next set of ten. It was involved and took him some time, but finally he was done.

He counted them.

"One hundred and fifty kilometers," he said. "One point six kilometers to a mile. Just under a hundred miles."

He looked at Derek, who did not move, who made no sign.

"There are people just under a hundred miles from here."

But what good did that do?

"Here it is—I could leave you and try to follow the river out and bring help back."

Which, he thought, sounded insane. There were animals. They would come, and if they thought Derek was dead. . . . He was defenseless. They might attack him. Even eat him. Even small things—ants, bugs.

"I can't leave you."

Brian looked at the map again. It was there, the answer was there. Brannock's Trading Post was the answer and the river was the answer, but he didn't see how.

He couldn't leave Derek.

He couldn't leave Derek. . . .

What if he took Derek with him?

He said it aloud. "What if we went out together?"

On the face of it, it sounded like madness. Haul a man in a coma nearly a hundred miles out of the wilderness on a river.

You could say that, Brian thought, but there was a lot of difference between saying it and doing it.

How could he?

The river. If he had a boat . . . or a raft.

If he made a raft and put Derek on the raft, there might be a way he could make the run and take Derek out, get him to the trading post and to help.

And even as he said it he knew it was crazy. A hundred miles on a wilderness river with a raft, hauling a grown man who would be nothing but dead weight, was impossible.

He would have dropped it, except that he looked up from the map and saw the truth then; looked up and saw Derek with his eyes half open and not seeing, awake but not truly living, the minutes of his life moving past and Brian knew that he really didn't have any choice.

If he stayed Derek would die of thirst in two, perhaps three days. Well before the week or ten days that would pass before the pilot came looking to see what happened.

If he stayed, Derek would die.

If he made the run, took Derek down the river, at least there was a chance.

He had no choice.

15

Time was everything now—once the decision was made, time was vital. But Brian took a minute to scan the map once more and do some mental calculating, and it didn't come up too terrible.

Say it was a hundred miles by river.

When they'd landed they'd come down next to where the river left the lake, and Brian had watched the current as it flowed away. It seemed to move about as fast as a person walked—maybe three miles an hour. Of course, that didn't mean that it would continue to flow at that speed, but it would probably be about the same.

If he could get into the current and move with it and stay with it, a hundred miles would take thirty-five or forty hours.

He studied it closer on the map and noted that it grew wider as it flowed and that in some places it moved through hilly country—there were contour lines on the map close together, which meant steeper hills. Here the current might even be a little faster.

A day and a half, he thought. Then he said it aloud for Derek. "A day and a half. A long day and a half, but if we keep moving, stay in the river and don't stop, we should make the trading post in a day and a half. Maybe two days." And that, he thought without saying, is a lot better than seven or eight.

A lot better than dying.

There were two places where the river ran into lakes and out the other end, and many smaller ponds and what might be swamps where the river moved through a center of a small body of water. They would slow him down.

He could not judge how much, but none of them were large, and if he stayed on the edge and used a pole he should be able to keep moving well enough not to lose too much time.

Time.

He was sitting, reading, looking at the map, and there wasn't time for it.

He needed to build a raft.

He checked Derek one more time, made certain his breathing was regular and that his heart was beating steadily and then moved off down the side of the lake, looking for wood.

The problem was not wood so much as the lack of a tool. When he'd made the raft before to go out to the plane he'd had his hatchet, and he missed it terribly now. After he'd been rescued and gone home, his mother had put the hatchet in a glass case in the living room, where she kept the china handed down by her grandmother. He'd looked at it as he'd left the house, but they had decided that having a hatchet might not be realistic.

"Lots of people carry a knife of some kind," Derek had said. "But how many have a hatchet on their belt?"

So all he had was a knife—well, two knives, actually. He had Derek's knife as well. He'd almost forgotten that.

But even two knives wouldn't help him cut through logs.

There was wood all over the place. Wind storms over the years had knocked down pines and spruce trees and many of them were the right diameter to use for making a raft—six or eight inches and straight. But they were for the most part too long, or still connected to the root structure, which made them impossible to use.

But Brian moved along the lake, up from the shore and back, and finally he found a stand of large poplars where beavers had been working.

He knew almost nothing of beavers except that they lived in the water, chewed trees down, and looked cute when he saw them swimming in the water. Except for pictures he'd never seen one on dry land, but he'd seen how they took trees down and this stand of poplars was a good example. In a hundred-yard circle there wasn't a tree standing.

There were pointed stumps everywhere, with tooth marks on them, and dropped trees fallen across each other so thickly that it looked like giants had started to play pick-up-sticks and walked away before finishing the game.

The beavers had been working at the grove for some time—probably years—and they had not only dropped the trees, many of them the right diameter, but they had cut the limbs off and dragged them down pathways to the lake and cut some of the tree trunks in sections between eight and ten or twelve feet long, apparently to make them easier to move.

It's like I hired them, Brian thought, looking at all the fallen poplars—just to cut them down for me.

The older trees, which had been cut down the year or two before, were well dried out, and when Brian rolled and skid-

ded them down to the lake he found that they floated wel
Four of them side by side held him up easily when he usc
his arms to hold them together and crawled on top of them.
He got wet, but they held him.

Of course, Derek was a lot heavier and the two of them together heavier still, but eight or ten of them should do it. And there were many the right size and length. He had only to select the ones he wanted.

He worked hard for a solid half hour, then ran to check on Derek. He was still the same, and Brian jogged back to the beavers' woodyard.

He picked eight logs, each running close to eight inches thick and roughly eight feet long. He selected the driest ones he could find, going by feel. He'd learned that from firewood. The drier, the lighter.

The wood was soft, felt soft to the point of his knife, and he thought that might mean they would waterlog, but then he decided it wouldn't matter. It would take weeks, or at least days, to soak into an eight-inch log, and he wouldn't need the logs that long.

One way or the other, he thought, while dragging the first log down to the lake.

The beavers had left clear sliding trails where they had dragged branches down to the lake, and Brian used one of them, the main trail, to pull the logs down. The last four feet to the water were fairly steep and the mud was slick from the recent rain and the logs pretty much made their own way to the lake, pushing him ahead down into the water.

He had a plan—or as much of a plan as he could have for what he was going to try to do. He couldn't move Derek very far by mere strength—he had to weigh close to a hundred and eighty pounds, compared to Brian's one-forty. Brian couldn't carry him and could only drag him a short distance.

So he had to bring the raft to just below the shelter—bring

the raft to Derek—and that meant building it here and working it up the side of the lake to Derek.

It took him less than an hour to get all the logs down to the water, and when he lay them side by side and lined the ends together he was pleased to see that they made a usable-looking raft. The ends weren't quite even, but close, and they were pointed, the way the beavers had chewed them off. It gave them a streamlined look.

Like something out of *Huckleberry Finn,* he thought.

Except that nothing held them together yet. Brian stood next to them in knee-deep water and studied the problem.

He had no rope, no string, and yet he had to have a way to hold the logs in a flat platform to keep them solid enough to carry Derek and him.

He had his clothing. His jacket—the same type windbreaker he'd had when he first had to survive after the plane crash—and he had Derek's jacket as well, though Brian wanted to keep that for cover for Derek.

But even cutting the jackets in strips might not make enough roping to tie all the logs together. He cast around, half looking for vines or grasses he could weave into a rope.

But again the beavers helped him. They had also cut smaller sticks—limbs and the tops of the trees—some of them five or six feet long and two or three inches in diameter.

They provided his answer. He made cross-pieces with them, put one on top and one on the bottom and sandwiched the raft body logs in place. Then he cut strips from his jacket and tied the two cross-pieces together at the ends so that they were pulled together and held the logs firmly in place. By using his knife to notch the cross-pieces to take the material, he made sure the cloth tie-downs didn't slip off.

He put four of these cross members down the length of the raft, tying them in place as tight as he could get them, and when he was done the raft was stout enough for him to stand on, jump on, walk back and forth on.

It was about eight feet long, five and a half feet wide, and floated well out of the water, and had not taken him more than two hours to build.

He had gone back twice to check on Derek while working and now that it was finished he cut a long pole for pushing the raft and used his knife to carve a crude paddle, then moved back to the camp before bringing the raft.

He was not hungry—still felt too nervous for hunger—but knew he should eat before they started or he would be too weak. So he ate nuts and some berries they had stored in a birch-bark cone, ate everything he could find in the shelter—they wouldn't need it on the run—and examined Derek closely one more time while he ate.

This whole thing, he knew, was crazy and had only a small chance of working. He knew that, understood that. If there was one thing he understood about working in an emergency—surviving—it was that there was a large measure of luck involved.

And if there was the slightest, tiniest change in Derek, any indication at all that he was coming out of it, Brian would call the trip off and hope for the best.

So he studied Derek, worked at it as hard as he could. He looked into the unconscious man's eyes and saw nothing, just the glazed look that was there before. He carefully measured his breathing and his heartbeat and found them to be the same—exactly—as they had been since he'd started to keep track of them.

He yelled into Derek's ear, looking for some reaction in the eyes, and there was no sign of any kind that he could hear, or that he could react to hearing.

Finally, he tried pain. He used the tip of his knife to poke Derek's hand, again watching the man's eyes and there was, simply, nothing—even when he poked hard enough to draw a small drop of blood.

No sign of any kind of life or knowledge except the breathing and the heartbeat.

Then he waited a few minutes and did it all again, working steadily, carefully, and it was the same. He had to be certain, absolutely certain that there was no choice.

And he was.

He stood and looked across the lake and felt strangely old. It was his decision to make and yet another man could die because of what he decided. He had never been in this position, and it frightened him. Even when he was in danger, even when he had to fight just to live, his decisions only affected him—never another person.

And now Derek lay there and Brian looked down to where he'd pulled the raft to the shore by the shelter and opened his mouth and said:

"We go." It came out as a whisper.

Right or wrong, they had to do it—Brian had to do it. *Please, God,* he thought—and did not finish it. Just that—please, God. He turned to face Derek and coughed and said it again, loud and clear.

"We go."

THE RIVER

16

It proved to be almost impossible to start.

Brian took the briefcase down to the raft, and decided to take a weapon—he left the bow but took two lances he had made. One fish spear with twin tines held open with a small stick that he had made to show Derek that you could use a spear as well as a bow to take small fish. The other was a straight spear with a fire-hardened point that he had decided to use if necessary on a moose.

"Did it really attack you?" Derek had asked, when he told of his time near the *L*-shaped lake and the moose attack. "Really come at you?"

"And stayed with it," Brian said. "I couldn't do anything—it just kept coming back, pushing me down underwater until I pretended to be dead. Next time I'm going to fight back."

So he had made the spear and hoped that he would never have to use it.

When the spears and the briefcase were on the raft, he went back to the camp.

Derek. The true reason for the raft. He had to get Derek down to the raft and on it without hurting him, or worse, drowning him.

He turned Derek onto his back, grabbed him under the shoulders, and tried to pull him down the bank.

Derek didn't move.

Brian pulled and the man just lay still, and Brian looked to see if his shoe had caught on a root by the fire or in the brush, but it had not.

It just couldn't be that hard to move a—he almost thought body—person. Just a person on his back. He ought simply to skid down the bank.

In the end Brian did get him to skid—about three inches at a time. He heaved and jerked and pulled until finally Derek was on the bank, lying on his side, facing the water.

There was a small ledge and a drop of approximately six inches to the water. This close in to the shore the lake was very shallow, not enough water to float the raft, and Brian had to horse the raft sideways to get it in so that it was lying sideways next to Derek and just below him, grounded on the mud of the bottom.

He kneeled in the water next to the raft. He had been soaked since starting to build the raft and figured to remain wet until . . . until they made it. He did not wish to think of the alternatives.

He used his hip to jam the raft into the bank and reached across to pull Derek onto the raft.

Again, it was like moving lead weight. Derek seemed bolted to the earth and Brian had to settle for pulling first one end, then the other, back and forth from Derek's arms to his ankles until the man was at last on the raft, which settled into the mud of the bottom under Derek's weight and remained solid.

Brian positioned him first on his back and then decided he might choke and moved him over onto his side, in the center of the raft. The middle cross-piece on the raft caught Derek in the soft part just above his hip and helped to hold him in place, but Brian did not think it would be enough. He tore more strips from his jacket and made a tie-down. This he used to go from one side of the raft, over Derek's shoulders to the other side, to tie him into position.

Finally, with Derek lashed in, Brian used Derek's own jacket rolled up to make a pillow, which he worked beneath Derek's head.

He checked the breathing and heartbeat again and he was surprised to see that he did it almost automatically. It had just been hours—just over a day and a half—and he was already reacting automatically.

"Derek, I don't know if you can hear me." He settled in the water next to the grounded raft and spoke to Derek's face. "I'm going to tell you anyway. We're going to take this raft down the river that leads from the lake. It's just under a hundred miles to a trading post. The thing is, we can't stay here because . . . well, it just wouldn't work. And the radio was blown by the same lightning that hit you. So we can't call for help. So we have to do this, we have to do this. . . ." He shook his head, choked, realized that he was close to crying. "Oh, hell, we just have to do this—I hope it works out."

He started to work the raft out of the mud and float it free when he thought of something.

What if they came unexpectedly?

If they just found Derek and Brian gone, they wouldn't know what to think.

He had to leave a note.

He opened the briefcase and took out a pencil and a notebook. He wrote in large, block letters.

Big storm.
Derek hit by lightning and in coma.
Trying to raft river down to
Brannock's Trading Post 100 miles
south. Come quick.

BRIAN ROBESON

He studied the note, then added the date and time. He had left the radio behind back up in the campsite, thinking it would be in the way. He ran back up to the shelter and found the radio in its plastic case and folded the note and put it in the case so that it stuck out slightly. Then he tied the radio back up under the overhang with its carrying strap so that anybody coming into the shelter would be certain to see it.

Back at the raft he found that Derek's weight had pushed it into the bottom so hard, it was difficult to get loose.

He sawed it back and forth, one end out, then the other and finally it broke free, though floating still in little more than a foot of water.

"Good place to test it," he said. It seemed very stable with just Derek on it and Brian carefully eased his knees onto the end by Derek's feet.

The end sank lower a few inches, but still was well above the surface. He raised on his knees and rocked back and forth, ready to jump off if it started over. The raft bobbed back to level and settled from the roll fast, the flat bottom slapping the water lightly.

"It's seaworthy." He climbed back off the raft and checked Derek again. He was resting in the same position. Some water had come up between the logs and made his shoulders wet, but his head was up on the jacket pillow and was still dry.

Brian looked at the sun.

It was mid-afternoon. Dark was still five or six hours away—not that it mattered. Once they started they would have to keep moving, even through the night if they could.

Time was everything.

The river left the lake at the south end, a good half mile away. Rather than try to move the raft across the lake, he decided to pull it around the edge in the shallows and he started moving along the shore.

The raft followed easily and Brian let himself feel just the slightest bit positive for the first time since the lightning had hit them.

The raft seemed to work well. The weather was holding. They had a map.

And most of all, Derek was still alive.

They had a shot at it.

17

Their luck held.

Where the river left the lake it cut a deeper channel in the soft bottom. It took Brian half an hour to move the raft down the side of the lake, pulling it along by hand, and where the river exited he moved to the left shore and stopped for a moment.

One last thought. He could still go back. It would be easy to take the raft back around the lake, and possible—though certainly not easy—to drag Derek back up to the shelter. Once they were on the river, with the current, he would not be able to work back.

But he hesitated only a moment. Any choosing was already finished and he shook his head.

It was done.

He climbed onto the back of the raft, kneeling at Derek's

feet as he had before, and used the pole to push it away from the bank and out into the current.

The river was sixty or seventy feet across, leaving the lake, and the current at the sides seemed a bit slower. It caught the raft and pulled the nose around, so it aimed downstream but along the edge, bouncing against the bank and sliding beneath overhanging willows and brush.

Brian used the pole—the bottom was four or five feet down—and pushed the raft sideways out into the center.

It hesitated, seemed to hold for a moment as if trying to find the current, then the moving water caught the logs and the raft started to move.

Inside of thirty feet it was matching the current, or close to it, and Brian watched the banks sliding past as the raft moved silently down the river.

"We're on the way," he said to Derek. "It's working and we're on the way."

For a hundred yards the river moved straight, then curved hard to the left around a small hill where Brian quickly found that a log raft is not the same as a boat.

The current was not fast—as he had guessed earlier it was about the speed of a person walking—but it was steady and strong. The logs were heavy and once they were moving in a direction they were hard to turn.

As a matter of fact, Brian thought, watching the bank at the end of the curve come at him, they were impossible to turn.

The river curved left and the raft went straight, cut across the curve, and jammed into the bank.

The jar of the sudden stop, even moving slowly, rocked the raft and Derek rolled against the lashings and almost fell in.

Brian leaped forward on the raft, fell on Derek and held him while the raft lurched, slid sideways, and settled against the bank, where it stuck in the dirt and brush on the edge of the river.

One hundred yards and they were stopped.

Brian slid off the raft—waist deep in the water—pushed it sideways back out into the current, climbed back on and sat for half a minute while the river curved back around to the right and the raft jammed into the left bank.

Another fifty yards. One hundred and fifty yards and they were stuck twice.

Brian swore.

"I'm going to have to improve this or we'll be a month on this river."

He worked the raft into the middle again and it started to move.

This time, as they came into a shallow curve and the raft started to move straight, he waited until the raft was close to the shore and used the pole to jam into the bottom and fend off.

He still shot wide on the turn, but they didn't jam into the bank and by the fifth curve he had found a way to use the crude paddle to steer the raft.

He would come in close to the shore on the inside of a curve, then as soon as the raft was around it he paddled the stern over and aimed it down the center of the river, and fought to keep it in the middle.

They still did not always stay in the center of the best-moving current, but as the afternoon wore on Brian found that by frantically paddling through each curve he kept the raft moving almost at the speed of the current and away from any brush or snags on the sides of the river.

It worked, but the river curved almost constantly, moving through small swamps and beneath overhanging trees so thick it seemed to be a jungle, and he was constantly fighting the raft.

Inside of three hours he felt his back and arms aching, and knew that if he didn't stop to rest a bit now and then he would never be able to make it.

He decided to stop every hour for ten minutes. Derek had told him once that that was what the military did on long marches—a ten-minute break every hour—and by the end of the fourth hour he was more than ready for it. As it happened the break came when the river straightened out, so he didn't lose any time. The raft kept sliding as he leaned back and rested his arms and back.

He used his hands to cup water into his face, rubbing the back of his neck. The evening sun was still hot when it hit him as they came out of the patches of shade made by the trees on the bank, and the cool water on his neck refreshed him.

"Let's see how we're doing." He opened the briefcase and took out the map. The river was accurately drawn—or seemed to be—and as near as he could figure it they'd come about eight miles.

Not as good as he'd thought. Eight miles in four hours. Two miles an hour. That meant fifty hours.

Two full days, on top of the day they'd just used making the decision and getting ready to go. Four days without water for Derek.

He looked at the unconscious form and saw that the sun had burned his neck where the skin was exposed.

Well, if Derek couldn't drink, Brian could still keep him cool. That might help.

He took his T-shirt off and soaked it in the water. Brian used it as a cloth to wipe Derek's face and neck with cool water during his break.

This ordeal was amazing to him, and he wondered at how it could be. Things happened so fast, changed so fast. Derek had been—*no,* he thought—Derek *was still* one of those people who seemed so . . . so alive. He was eager to learn, happy, bright.

He seemed indestructible.

Even now, lying on his side on the raft in the evening light —his chest rising and falling as he breathed—he looked like he would wake up any second.

Cut down—that's how Brian thought of him. He had read a history of the Civil War and the author had written about the men being "cut down by fire."

That's how Derek looked to Brian now—cut down. How could that be?

Here he was, no different really, had been in the same place at the same time and he was all right, and Derek was cut down.

He wiped Derek's face several times. All this time the raft had kept moving, and when his break was over he saw that they were coming into another bend.

He put the T-shirt back on, wet, and picked up the paddle and started to work, swinging the stern of the raft, keeping it in the middle of the current.

It would be dark in an hour or so, but he thought that it wouldn't matter. His hands were raw from the rough wood of the paddle and he thought that it wouldn't matter either.

All that mattered now was to keep moving.

18

In the night, that first night, he learned some things about himself.

Not all of them were good.

He had not slept the night before except to doze kneeling next to Derek, and he had worked hard all day on the raft getting it ready, and when the sun went down and the darkness caught him he could not believe how much he wanted to sleep.

There was a partial moon—a sliver—which gave enough light to see the river, or at least make out the main channel, but the light didn't help.

Each time Brian's eyes closed to blink, they opened more slowly, and each time he had to fight to get them open.

The mosquitoes helped for a time. They came out in their clouds with darkness before the evening cool slowed them and Brian tried brushing them away from his face and Derek's, but it was like trying to brush smoke. As soon as his hand passed they settled again, whining in the darkness and after a bit he just let them eat and kept paddling.

Sleep would take him between strokes of the paddle; it would stop him so his arms would fall and the paddle would stop and lay in his lap. Then he would shake his head and snap out of it and start paddling again just in time to make a turn, at least at first. Halfway through the night nothing worked anymore and his eyes closed and stayed shut.

He dreamed mixes of things.

His mother came to him, sitting on the other end of the raft.

"It's all right," she said. "You can let go now—it's all right."

And her voice was so soft, so gentle and soothing that he *wanted* to let all of it go, not to be here. Not even in the dream.

He was not sure how long he slept, but when he awakened the raft was drifting on a large, flat plain of water, bobbing sideways.

There was no sign of the river.

In the faint moonlight he could see no banks, knew no direction to travel.

"But . . ." he said aloud. The sound of his voice startled some animal and there was a loud splashing to his right.

A large animal, he thought—perhaps a moose. That meant there was a shore, then, a bank for an animal to run on—close.

So use thought, use logic. Use it. Think.

The river was flowing generally southeast. It must have widened into a lake.

The moon.

The moon was straight overhead when he went to sleep.

Now it was down a ways to the right.

Down to the west. Like the sun it rose in the east, set in the west.

The moon was about halfway down from overhead in the same direction as the splashing animal.

So.

Brian threw water in his face.

So the river had widened into a lake, but he had moved along the west bank. If he kept moving the raft with the paddle he should come to where the river narrowed again, and pick up the current.

He started paddling, the raft moving sluggishly now that there was no real current. He bore to the right, moving the raft sideways as he paddled until he could just make out the shoreline in the darkness—outlined in the moonlight—then he straightened and started paddling again, steady, reaching forward with each stroke, bending at the waist, two on the right, two on the left.

While the raft followed current well, because the logs stuck down into the water and were not streamlined, for the same reason it moved with the paddling horribly.

"It's like paddling a brushpile," he said to Derek. "Nothing seems to move."

And in truth it was very slow. He was not moving more than a mile an hour and he wished he could read the map in the darkness. He didn't remember this lake, or wide place, or whatever it was, but if it was two miles long it would take two full hours at least to cross it.

Two on the left, two on the right.

He slogged forward and with the rhythm of the paddling his brain settled into numbness again and soon he was in the same trance that had led him to sleep.

This time he stayed awake, but the hallucinations grew more and more intense.

He saw the raft as a canoe and felt it fly forward with each stroke until he was leaving a wake of fire, firewaves curling out from the front of the raft and he worried that it would catch the logs/canoe on fire and burn them up and how could water be on fire anyway?

He would shake his head and then see his mother again at the other end of the raft. She would change into his father, who was smiling and beckoning him to paddle faster and faster; and then Derek's breath grew louder and louder until it filled his head, the lake, the world with the rasping sound of his breathing, and Brian could hear Derek's heart as well, pounding on the logs of the raft, echoing until all he could hear was the keening rasp of Derek's breath and the pounding of his heart. . . .

He would shake his head and the raft would be jerking forward in the faint moonlight, Derek lying on his side, Brian leaning forward at the waist, two on the left, two on the right, the paddle pulling at the water in swirls. Three strokes, four, and he would be under again.

At one point something came swimming up alongside the raft—a muskrat or otter or beaver—cutting a *V* in the water as it swam next to Brian, and in a fraction of a second his mind had turned it into the head of some beast, some underwater monster with its toothed head weaving back and forth getting ready to attack, to sweep over and take him off the raft with huge teeth; and he set the paddle down and grabbed for the spear to kill the monster, make it go away before it could eat him, and he shook his head and the vision disappeared as the animal dived and the monster was gone and he was alone with Derek again. He picked up the paddle and worked again, leaning forward. . . .

The bad thinking came sometime toward morning. He did not know how it started and would never know how it started and, later, did not wish to remember it when he did.

Two nights without sleep tore at him and the raft seemed bolted down as he tried to get it along the edge of the lake to where the river moved again. Somewhere there, as he tried to keep the raft moving and fought sleep, there came the idea, the wild idea, the sick idea.

The raft moved slowly because it was heavy. What made it heavy, sank it into the water so that it could not move, was the extra weight of the man tied in the middle. If the man were gone—if the man were gone it would be lighter and he could move fast and it would be better.

It would be better if Derek were gone. What was the difference? He was dumb enough to rise up and get hit by the lightning, and he should be gone.

Brian looked down at the still form and thought the thought; and it was so awful that he did not believe he was thinking it, but it was there, the thought.

If Derek were gone.

Just gone.

None of this would have happened if Derek weren't there —not any of it. And if Derek were gone . . . gone somehow in the water, gone down and down. . . .

"No!" He nearly screamed it and the sound of his voice snapped him awake, alert, and he touched Derek's leg to make certain he was still there, that Brian hadn't cut him loose in the night and that he would always be there and that Brian would never even think the thought again. Not even for an instant.

"All the way," he mumbled, reaching with the paddle again. "We go all the way together."

He paddled another half hour, fighting sleep and then at the same time he felt a coolness that he knew was morning coming and he saw that the eastern sky was beginning to lighten.

He stopped paddling, looked at the sky and was amazed at

how fast the dawn came. One moment it was so dark he couldn't see Derek on the raft and the next he could make out the bank, see the trees in the gray light of dawn.

And they were moving.

The banks were moving along, even though he wasn't paddling. He'd done it, he was through the lake and had moved back onto the river and the current had him.

"Thank you," he whispered, and realized when he said it that it was another kind of prayer and that he was grateful not just for the river, the current, the movement—but the other thing as well.

Coming through the night with Derek . . . grateful that he had made it.

"Thank you."

19

With the arrival of good light Brian took the map out and spread it on the briefcase.

The lake he had crossed did not show. He was positive. There were lakes, some large and small, but he was not moving fast enough to have reached any of them yet and that meant the map was not accurate.

It showed clean river with narrow banks where he guessed the lake to be and if it was inaccurate about this one thing then it might be wrong about all things.

Say the distance to the trading post. If the map had been made many years before and not updated, then the river might have changed direction, might not even go by the trading post any longer.

The trading post might not even be there.

The thought stunned him and he realized how foolish it

had been to leave the lake and trust the map. There were so many variables, so many ways to go wrong.

He studied the map again and took some heart from it. It was so . . . so definite. It must be basically right. Close. Things could change, but not that much. The river was probably up a bit and the lake he had come through in the night was a low place that filled when the river ran high and not really a permanent lake that would be on the map.

Sure. There was logic there. All right. All he had to do was test the map, find some way to ensure that it was mostly right.

He put his finger on the river and followed it, tracing the path as the blue line cut through the green, followed it to where he thought he must be.

There.

If the map was right and he was guessing right, he should be about where his finger had stopped. It showed a long straight stretch and the contour lines were spread far apart, which would indicate a large low or flat area where there might be a lake.

Better yet, in a short distance—less than two miles—the contour lines came closer and closer together and showed two hills, one on either side of the river, just after a sharp *S* turn.

The raft was moving well now and the morning sun was cutting away some of the ache and tiredness of the night. He put the map back in the briefcase and checked on Derek. His face was swollen from the mosquitoes in the night, his eyes puffy and shut, and Brian used his T-shirt to wipe cool water on Derek's face. He rinsed it in the river and dampened Derek's mouth with fresh, clean water.

He wasn't sure if his eyes were being tricked or if it was real, but Derek looked thinner to him and he wondered if getting thinner was a sign of dehydration.

He dampened the T-shirt once more and put it over Derek's head. If he stays cool, Brian thought, cool and moist, it might help. If I can keep him out of the sun. . . .

If the raft had a canopy, a cover, it would help. He paddled to the shore and jammed the raft into some willows and grass. It took him a half hour to use some green willows and swatches of grass to arrange a crude awning over Derek. It did not cover the whole man, but kept most of him in shade, and when it was done Brian pushed the raft back out into the current and started moving again.

He watched for the hills. Hunger came with the morning and he started thinking about food. Cereal and milk, toast, bacon, fried eggs—the smells of breakfast seemed to hang over the raft.

It bothered him, but it was an old friend/enemy. He made himself quit thinking of food, thought instead of what to do, planning each move of the day.

Get a firm location, figure his speed, keep moving—a step at a time.

Time.

Time was so strange. It didn't mean anything, then it meant everything. It was like food. When he didn't have it he wanted it, when there was plenty of it he didn't care about it.

He stretched, sighed. "You know, if we were in a canoe and had a lunch and a cooler full of pop, we'd think this was the most beautiful place in the world."

And it was, he thought, truly beautiful. The trees, pines and spruce and cedars, towered so high they made the river seem to become narrow and in places where the bank was cut away by the moving water the trees had actually leaned out over the river until they were almost touching. They made the river seem like a soft, green tunnel.

The character of the river had changed. It happened almost suddenly, but with such a natural flow that Brian didn't notice it for a short time. The trees grew closer, the brush thicker and the banks higher.

Where they had been grassy and sloping away gradually, the banks were steeper and cut away, exposing the dirt and mud. The trees were so close and high that Brian would not be able to see the hills on the map when he came to them. He could see nothing but a wall of green.

He wiped Derek's face several times. All this time the raft had kept moving, and when his break was over he saw that they were coming into another bend.

He put the T-shirt back on, wet, and picked up the paddle and started to work, swinging the stern of the raft, keeping it in the middle of the current.

It would get hot soon and cook him, but he thought that it wouldn't matter. His hands were raw from the rough wood of the paddle and he thought that it wouldn't matter either.

All that mattered now was to keep moving.

20

He saw the hills from the map sooner than he thought he should see them.

But they were the right ones. He was sure of it. They rose steeply ahead and on either side, rounded but high, covered with trees.

It was just about noon and the sun was beating down on him. He reached under the shelter and used the damp T-shirt to cool Derek again.

"We're moving," he said, his voice thick with exhaustion, not believing it. "We're moving along now. . . ."

And when he said it he knew it was true. The raft was increasing in speed. Even as he watched, the speed seemed to pick up.

"We're hauling. . . ." He started, then trailed off as it dawned on him.

The contour lines being close together on the map meant that the banks steepened between the hills.

If there were hills and steep banks, the river might drop, fall a bit.

He reached for the briefcase to take another look at the map, but stopped with his hand halfway out.

A sound.

Some sound was there that at first he could not place. It was so soft, he could almost not hear it at all over the sounds of the birds.

But there it was again. A hissing? Was that it?

No.

It was lower than that. Not to be heard, but felt.

A *whooshing*—water.

A water sound.

A rumbling sound. The sound of water moving fast, dropping, falling.

Falling water.

A waterfall.

They were heading for a waterfall!

21

There was no time left. The river had narrowed slightly, but now there was more of a drop and the speed had increased dramatically.

They were dead in the middle of the river and Brian knew he had to get to shore, had to stop, but there was no time.

Twice as fast as he could walk, the raft was fairly careening now.

The sound was louder.

If he tried to paddle for shore, he would succeed only in turning the raft sideways. He was not sure how he could get over a waterfall—if indeed he could at all—but he was fairly certain he did not want to try it with the raft sideways. If it went the long way over the waterfall, it would be harder to roll over. Sideways and it would roll easily.

The sound was a definite rumble now, and in seconds they wheeled around a bend and Brian could see it.

"God . . ."

It was a whisper.

It was not a waterfall, but it might as well have been.

The river moved between two large stone bluffs that formed the sides of the two hills Brian had seen on the map.

The bluffs forced the river to a narrower width, deeper, and at the same time aimed it through some boulders that had split off either side and dropped in the middle.

All of this had the effect of making a monstrous chute where the water fought and roared to get through, smashing around the rocks in huge sprays of white water.

And the raft was aimed right down the middle of the chute.

Things happened so fast after that, there was not a way he could prepare for it.

The raft seemed to come alive, turn into a wild, crazy animal.

The front end took the river, swung down and into the current, grabbed the madness of the water and ran with it.

Brian had just time to look down at Derek, just time to see that he was still tied to the raft securely, and they were into it.

The raft bucked and tore at the water, slammed sideways. Brian tried to steer, using the paddle to swing the stern to the left and right, trying to avoid the boulders, but it was no use.

The water owned the raft, owned Derek, owned him. In the roaring, piling thunder of the river he had no control.

They were flying, the logs of the raft rearing out of the water on pressure ridges, slamming back down so hard it rattled his teeth.

In the middle of the chute was a boulder—huge, gray, wet with waves and spray—and the raft aimed directly at the center of it.

He had time to scream—sound lost in the roar of water—

and throw himself on Derek. The raft wheeled slightly to the left and struck the boulder.

Brian thought for part of a second that they had made it.

Derek's body lurched beneath him and dropped back, the raft took the blow, flexed, gave, but held together; and Brian started one clear thought: we made it.

Then it hit. There was an underwater boulder next to the giant in the middle of the river. Hidden by a pressure wave, it lay sideways out and to the left, halfway to the left wall.

The nose of the raft made it, carried over by the pressure ridge, hung for a second, then dropped, plummeted down.

As it tipped forward the rear of the raft cut down into the water and came against the submerged ledge.

"Whunk!"

Brian heard it hit, felt the impact and the sound through his whole body. He grabbed, tried to hold on to the logs beneath Derek, but it was no use.

The stern kicked off the ledge, slapped him up and away, clear of the raft, completely in the air.

He hung for a split instant in midair, looking down on the raft, on Derek—then he plunged down, down into the boiling, ripping water.

Everything was madness—frothy green bubbles, hissing, roiling water.

He came up for a moment, saw the raft shooting away downstream carrying Derek, then he was down again, mashed down and tumbled by the pressure wave, smashed into the rocks on the bottom, and all he could think was that he had to stay alive, had to get up, get air, get back to the raft.

But the wave was a great weight on him, a house on him; the world was on him and he could not move up against it.

He fought and clawed against the rock, broke his face free, then was driven down again, hammered into the bottom.

Sideways.

He'd have to work sideways. Smashed, buffeted, he dragged himself to the side beneath the pressure wave.

It became stronger. He could not rise, could not get air, and his lungs seemed about to burst, demanded that he breathe, even if it was water. He willed the urge away, down, but it grew worse, and just when he knew it was over, when he would have to let the water in—when he would die—just then he made the edge of the pressure wave at the side of the boulder.

The current roared past the rock and took him like a chip, sucking him downstream.

He brought his head clear for one tearing breath, opened and shook water out of his eyes long enough to see that the raft was gone, out of sight—then he was driven back under, down to the bottom, smashing into boulders in a roaring green thunder, end over end until he knew nothing but the screaming need to breathe, to live, and then his head smashed into something explosively hard and he thought nothing at all.

22

Bright light flashed inside Brian's eyes—red and glaring—and he opened them to find that he was on his back, staring directly at the sun.

"Ecchh!" He rolled onto his stomach and spit and nearly choked on water.

He was in the shallows below the rapids, caught up in a small alcove in the shoreline.

The water was six or seven inches deep, with a gravel bottom. His senses returned and with them came the realization that he was all right. He was bruised, but nothing was broken; he had taken a little water, but apparently had coughed it out.

He was all right.

Derek.

The word slammed into him. Somehow, he had forgotten. . . .

He stood—his legs were a bit wobbly, but they held—and looked down the river.

It stretched away for half a mile, becoming more calm and peaceful as it dropped, nestled in trees and thick brush, a blue line in a green background. Birds flew across the water, ducks swam. . . .

There was no raft.

Brian turned, stood dripping, looking upriver into the rapids.

From below they did not look as bad. The pressure waves appeared smaller—even the boulder didn't seem as large. There was still the sound of the water—although that, too, was muted.

But there was no raft.

No Derek.

"Derek!"

He yelled, knowing it was futile.

He looked downriver again. There was no way the raft would have stopped in the rapids. It had to have come down, floated on downstream.

What had he seen? He frowned, trying to remember what had happened.

Oh, yes—the wave. The big submerged rock and the wave, the great wave had taken the raft and he had seen that—the raft moving off downriver. He did not think it had tipped; he seemed to remember that it was upright.

But Derek—was he still on the raft? He couldn't remember for certain, but it seemed that he was—everything was so confused. Tumbling in the rapids seemed to have shaken his brain loose.

He fought panic.

Things were—were what they were. If the raft rolled or if Derek fell off the raft, then . . . well then, that was it.

If not, Derek might still be all right.

"I have to figure he's still alive."

And if Derek was still on the raft, still alive, he was downriver.

Brian had to catch him, catch the raft.

He started to move along the bank, and did well for fifty or so yards. The bottom was gravel—spilled out by the rapids—but then it ended.

The river moved rapidly back into flatter country, swamps, lakes, and the first thing that happened was the bottom turned to mud.

Brian tried to move to the bank and run, but the brush was so thick and wild that it was like a jungle—grass, willows, and thick vines grabbed at him, holding him.

He moved back into the river—where the mud stopped him. If he tried to walk, when his weight came down, his feet sunk and just kept on going—two, three feet. The mud was so thick it pulled his right tennis shoe off, and when he groped to find it the mud held his arm, seemed to pull at him, tried to take him down.

He lost the shoe, clawed back to the bank and knew there was only one way to chase the raft.

"I'll have to swim."

But how far?

It didn't matter, he thought—Derek was down there somewhere. Brian had to catch him.

He shook his head, took off his remaining shoe, and left it on the bank.

He kept his pants on—they were not so heavy—and entered the river, pushed away from the bank until he was far enough out to start floating a bit.

He kicked off the mud and began to swim. Within three strokes he knew how tired he was—his whole body felt weak and sore from the beating he'd taken in the rapids.

But he could not stop. He worked along the edge, half swimming, half pushing along with his feet in the mud.

Downriver.

He had to catch the raft.

23

He became something other than himself that afternoon.

When he began to swim—after he'd overcome the agony of starting and his muscles had loosened somewhat—he tried to think.

The raft would move with the current, if it did not get hung up.

Brian would also move with the current, plus he had the added speed of swimming, and he should gain rapidly.

But when he rounded that first bend and did not see the raft, and cleared the next bend two hundred yards further on and did not see the raft, worry took him.

He stopped at the side and stood as much as he could in the mud.

It was nearly a quarter of a mile to the next bend and there was no raft.

Every muscle in his body was on fire. He slipped back into the water and began swimming again, taking long, even strokes, kicking and pushing along the mud; pulling himself forward.

Another bend, and another, always reaching, and always Brian's eyes sought the still form, the thatched top of the raft.

Nothing.

The river seemed to have swallowed Derek. Altogether he rounded six shallow bends and still there was no raft, the stupid raft that had hung up on every bend when he was trying to steer it and now perversely held the center of the river somehow. There was nothing but the green wall along either side, the trees that grew higher and higher now that the rock hills were passed, until they nearly closed over the top of the river; the green wall that closed in and covered him as he slid along the water, wanting to scream, but pulling instead, always pulling, a stroke, then another stroke, until there was not a difference between him and the water, until his skin was the water and the water was him, until he *was* the river and he came to the raft.

He nearly swam past it.

Brian moved near some willows, his face down in the water, reaching with his left arm and when he raised his head he was looking at the raft.

It had somehow come through all the bends and curves, and here must have caught a slight crosscurrent. The raft had moved to the outside of a shallow curve and had glided back beneath some overhanging willows and low trees.

All that showed was the rear end of the raft—and the bottom of Derek's shoes.

"Derek!"

Brian's hand had almost brushed the raft, but had he not looked up at the exact point that he had, he would have missed it.

He grabbed the raft, pulled himself up alongside.

Derek lay still, though his body had moved, twisted sideways on the raft.

"Derek," he said again, softer.

Derek's head was still to the side, the eyes half open, but if he had been pushed underwater in the rapids, even for a moment, it might be too late.

"Derek."

He looked done, gone, dead.

Brian tried his wrist, but could feel no pulse. He watched Derek's chest but it didn't seem to move. He leaned down put his ear against Derek's mouth, held his breath.

There.

Softly on his ear, a touch of breath—once, then again, small puffs of air.

"Derek." He was alive, still alive.

It was as if everything came loose in Brian at the same time. His body, his mind, his soul were all exhausted and he fell across Derek, asleep or unconscious, fell with his legs still in the water.

"Derek."

24

Suddenly he was paddling.

His eyes were open and he was kneeling in back of Derek and he was leaning forward with the paddle and he did not have the slightest idea of how he'd come to be there.

He had a new paddle in his hands, carved roughly from a forked branch with a piece of Derek's pantleg pulled across the fork to form the face of the paddle. Brian was moving the raft and the sun was shining down on him and it was all, everything, completely new to him.

A different world.

"I must have slept, then moved in my sleep. . . ."

The briefcase was gone—torn off in the rapids—and with it the map. Not that it mattered.

The banks were just all green and the river went ahead to the next bend. The trees hung over the top and there was nothing to see but a slot of sky and the water ahead and the endless, endless green.

Nothing to match with a map.

He could no longer think anyway. He had no idea how far they had come, how many hours or days they had been traveling or how far it still was to the trading post. He could only pull now, only pull with the paddle.

He knew absolutely nothing, except the raft and the paddle and his hands, which had gone beyond bleeding now and were sores that stuck to the shaft of the crude paddle; knew nothing but the need, the numbing, crushing need to get Derek somewhere, somewhere, somewhere down the river. . . .

Food, hunger, home, distance, sleep, the agony of his body—none of it mattered anymore.

Only the reach.

The bend forward at the waist, the pull back with the arms, two on the left, two on the right.

Two left.

Two right.

Two.

Two.

Into that long day and that long night he moved the raft, so beyond thought now that even the hallucinations didn't come; nothing was there but the front of the raft, Derek, and the river.

The river.

Sometime in the morning of the next day, any day, a thousand days or eight days—he could not tell—somewhere in that morning the river widened and made a sweeping curve to the left, widened to half a mile or more, and he saw or thought he could see a building roof, a straight line in the trees that did not look natural and then he heard it, the sound of a dog barking—not a wolf or coyote, but a dog.

There was a small dock.

People had dogs that barked, and they had docks. He kept pulling, still not able to think or do anything but stroke, pulled to the edge of the river until the raft nudged against the dock, bounced, and then the paddle dropped.

He was done.

Above him on the bank he saw a small brown and white dog barking at him, its tail jerking with each bark, the hair of his back raised. As Brian watched, the round face of a young boy appeared next to the dog.

"Help. Help me," Brian thought he said, but heard no sound. The face of the boy disappeared and in moments two more people came, a man and woman, and they ran down to the dock and looked down at Brian and he was crying up at them, his torn hands hanging at his sides down in the water, down in the river.

The river.

"Derek. . . ."

Hands took him then, hands pulled him onto the dock; and the man jumped in the water and untied Derek and took him as well.

Hands.

Strong hands to help.

It was over.

MEASUREMENTS

Brian, Derek, and the raft traveled one hundred and nineteen miles down a river with an average current speed of two miles an hour, in just under sixty-three hours.

When Brian started, the raft weighed approximately two hundred pounds, but soaking up water all the way, it nearly doubled its weight by the time they reached the trading post —which was actually nothing more than a small cabin on the river where trappers could bring their furs. The post was owned and manned by a husband, wife, and one small boy, but they had a good radio and could call for help.

Derek's coma was low grade, and in truth he probably would have been all right even if Brian had not made the run —although he would have suffered significantly from dehydration. He began to come out of the coma in another week and had fully recovered within six months.

During the run Brian lost twelve pounds, mostly in fluids,

though he drank river water constantly to make up for it, and his hands became infected from bacteria in the water. He healed rapidly—his hands became amazingly tough—and strangely suffered no real long-range difficulties from the run down the river, probably because his earlier time—the Time—had taught him so well.

His mother and father vowed never to let him go in the woods again, but relented after some little time when Brian pointed out that of all people who *were* qualified to be in the wilderness, he was certainly one of them.

About seven months after the incident, Brian was sitting alone at home wondering what to cook for dinner when the doorbell rang, and he opened the door to find a large truck parked in the street in front of the house.

"Brian Robeson?" the driver asked.

Brian nodded.

"Got some freight for you."

The driver went to the rear of the truck, opened it, and pulled out a sixteen-foot Kevlar canoe, with paddles taped to the thwarts. It was a beautiful canoe, light and graceful, with gently curving lines that made it look wonderfully easy to paddle.

Written in gold letters on each side of the bow were the words:

THE RAFT

"It's from a man named Derek Holtzer," the driver said, setting the canoe on the lawn. "There's a note taped inside."

He climbed back in the truck and drove away and Brian found the note.

"Next time," he read aloud, "it won't be so hard to paddle. Thanks."

1

David Alspeth stopped at the locked gate, felt in his hands the weight of the small box which he could not stand to see yet, looked down on the sailboat, and tried not to cry.

She was twenty-two feet long, with a two-foot wooden bowsprit sticking from her nose, a stainless steel pulpit above it. Her mast and boom were made of wood, kept in good shape and varnished to a high sheen. And she had stainless steel lifelines all around and a small cabin in the middle with two plastic portholes on each side.

She was old, designed by a man named Schock and made in the mid-sixties, so old her fiberglass hull had lost its shine and had a faintly sanded, opaque look to it, although the original color—a robin's-egg blue—still shone in the California sun. She had been made before they fully understood fiberglass and learned they could make it thin, so her hull was a full half inch thick, and somehow it made her look stout—tough and short and low and punchy and stout.

Across her stern was a wooden plaque and on it was hand carved *FROG*.

David ran his hand over his face. The *Frog*, he thought—and she's mine. I'm fourteen years old and I've got my own sailboat, my own complete sailboat and I would give everything, all that I am, to not have it. He looked out across the small marina that comprised most of the Ventura harbor.

There was a stiffening breeze kicking up the waves beyond the breakwaters and he smiled thinking of what his uncle Owen called waves.

"Lumps," he used to say when they were getting ready to go out and the wind was blowing the sea around. "The ocean is full of lumps. . . ."

And there it was—*used to say*. His uncle Owen didn't say anything now. Not anymore. His uncle Owen was dead. Oh God, he thought—this just stinks. It just stinks to have it be this way. He cradled the wooden box in one hand and pulled a plastic card out of his back pocket and looked at it.

3

It was a Ventura marina lock card made out to Owen Alspeth. He put the card in the slot next to the gate, heard the lock click, pulled the gate open. The tide was out and the walkway sloped down at a steep angle so that he had to hold the handrail to keep from trotting forward.

At the bottom the dock was flat, and he walked to the slip holding the *Frog*. She wasn't locked. Owen didn't believe in locks, didn't believe in anything that held or confined things.

"If they're going to steal something the lock won't stop them," he'd said. And nobody had ever stolen from him, though other boats in the marina had been hit several times. Didn't believe in locks or chains or tying things down. Ahh, David thought and he shook his head and tried to shake his grief, the memory of the whole stinking mess pouring back into his thoughts.

Owen had felt a backache and gone to the doctor on a Monday morning and by Tuesday he knew he was going to die, knew that the cancer he had would kill him, that they could do nothing. Nothing for him. Again David controlled the tears. Down the dock a bit an older man stared at him for a moment, then turned away.

It had spread so fast. The cancer—so incredibly fast. A week after he'd gone into the hospital they had found more tumors in his brain and Owen called

David in to visit him. David had wanted to go sooner but while they were running tests Owen had asked him to wait. David's parents—Owen was his father's brother—were taking turns staying with him in the hospital. His mother had been there when David came the first time, and Owen had asked her to leave.

David hated hospitals, and it was worse when he saw Owen lying in bed. He looked weak, caved in, dead already, dead and done, and when David saw him he was overwhelmed with the change. His uncle's cheeks were sunken and his whole face was cast in a gray that somehow looked even and flat. And the smell from him was a mixture of alcohol and urine and feces—David had heard his mother say that the tumor in his spine kept him from controlling himself from the waist down.

Instantly, without a single thought that it was coming, David threw up, and of course that made it all the more horrible. Owen, his Owen who was so close, his own Owen who had taken him out sailing so many times and who always kept himself so neat that when the wind blew his hair didn't move, his own sweet uncle Owen—and he couldn't see him without throwing up, making a mess all over the floor. To make it still worse Owen laughed. A skull laugh.

"Some smell, isn't it?"

And David thought, What can I say? What words

can come out now to make this all right? And of course nothing came and he stood there with the mess on his shirt and the floor, looking but trying not to stare, hurting and trying not to breathe, and he was taken by such a roar of hate that it made his vision blur even more than the tears.

There had to be somebody to hit for this, he thought—there had to be some damn enemy to hit for this, this stinking death thing that was in the room.

"They think I might make two more weeks," Owen said, shrugging, his bony shoulders like two hooks. Tubes seemed to be poked into him in many places and they rattled when he moved. "I doubt I'll make a week but who am I to know?"

David shook his head—angry jerks. "Don't talk like that, dammit. Things happen. People make it. There are things they can do. There are always things they can do. . . ."

But they both knew that the doctors could do nothing, could take nothing more from him nor add anything to him to save him.

"All they can do now is keep me drugged up and comfortable." Owen looked past David, out the window at the hills in back of Ventura. The smog-haze was thickening and the rolling, brush-covered hills were bathed in yellow muck. "I want you to have the *Frog*."

Another violent shake. "No. I can't take her. Not like this, not this way. You love that boat, you live for it. . . ." David trailed off, paused, finished lamely. "I just can't. It wouldn't be right."

Owen turned a dial on a small box at the edge of the bed. A tube ran from the box to a needle that entered his arm. He had a pinched look at the corners of his eyes, from the pain, but it lessened almost instantly. "It's a drug computer," he said, sighing. "It drips morphine into me and I can turn it up when the pain waves up. That's all there is now for me, little victories like that. I can turn a dial and soften pain. My whole life has come down to that. . . ."

Another silence. David was crying openly now, thinking of Owen. Once he had seen Owen dancing at a beach party with a heavy girl, and he had picked her up and held her while he danced in the sand, holding her like a feather, laughing, his arms and legs strong and tight, and now . . . now he seemed about to break from the weight of the sheets. Owen reached slowly to the nightstand next to the hospital bed, the increased drug dosage hitting him, and David saw now that there was a small envelope there. Owen scrabbled for it with his boned fingers, caught it, and handed it to David.

"Here is the title, signed over to you. You know how hard it is to find a notary public in a hospital? And the marina card is there. I think she still has some water in the tank, and there are some cans of food I left from my last trip to Catalina. I need a favor from you."

"Anything." And he meant it. I will die for you if it will save you. Anything.

"I am going to be cremated. I want you to take my ashes out alone on the *Frog*, out to sea alone, and leave me there. Take me to where you can't see land and scatter my ashes there on the water. . . ."

David held the envelope crushed in his hand, held it while he cried and the silence had come again, come and stayed and grown until David's mother came back into the room and broke it with talk.

He didn't make a week.

Just six days. On the fifteenth of May, while David was in his last day of school in the eighth grade, his uncle Owen died in a drugged state resembling a coma. Even knowing it was coming hadn't helped. The grief tore at David and his parents. Owen had no other family, had never married and had stayed close to them, lived only four blocks away, ate with them and was the first to take David sailing. Several times he had taken him on two- and three-day trips out to Santa Cruz Island and once to Catalina, and now he was suddenly gone.

Completely gone.

David stepped on the boat, felt her rock quickly to his weight, jerking lightly against the ropes that held her to the slip-dock. Seagulls had been perching on the boom; there was a mess on the top of the cabin and the floor of the cockpit, and he stepped to the side to miss it.

He unhooked the hasp holding the sliding cabin top hatch in place and slid it forward. His nose was immediately filled with the rank odor from inside the boat. The cabin hadn't been opened since the last time Owen had come to the marina, over a month ago, and it smelled of mustiness and mildew and fungus and something else as well, something David could not pin down at first.

When it came, finally, it stopped him cold, one hand on the top of the hatch. It was the smell of Owen. No. More than that. It was Owen himself. The ghost of Owen. The smell was the boat and Owen, and David could not tell in his mind where the boat ended and Owen began.

He sat then, on the edge of the cockpit, holding the box, and cried and cried, letting it roll out of him in uncontrollable heaves, his hands clasped between his knees and the sound of the waves and gulls and sea around him.